A CHILD OF THE COLD WAR

CODE NAME: KITTEN

CATHY O'BRYAN

A CHILD OF THE COLD WAR
CODE NAME KITTEN

Copyright © 2020 Cathy O'Bryan

eBook 978-1-7347818-0-9
Print book 978-1-7347818-1-6

All rights reserved. Except for use in any review, the reproduction or utilization of this work in whole or in part in any form by any electronic, mechanical or other means, now known or hereinafter invented, including xerography, photocopying and recording, or in any information storage or retrieval system, is forbidden without the written permission of the publisher.

This is a work of fiction. Names, characters, places and incidents are either the product of the author's imagination or are used fictitiously, and any resemblance to actual persons, living or dead, business establishments, events or locales is entirely coincidental.

Printed in the USA.

ONE

The Awakening

———▶———

NO ONE WAS KILLED EXCEPT the driver. I changed that day. Even though the weather had produced a beautiful October day with this moment the day seemed bleak. The explosion not only scared me, well terrified, me. I began to wake up as a person. Begining to shed my skin as a little kid that moment in October 1965. I am thirteen, thin as a rail but athletic due to my cherished dance classes. I *had* been only interested in the Beatles' new song "Yesterday", a good burger, and my fashion magazines. Now, maybe I should pay more attention to the real adult world. The USSR's Luna 7 crashing on the moon not to mention their nuclear tests was on the news last night. Even my teachers, having us practice bomb drills by climbing under our desks. Like that would help. What does all of that mean to me? Time, to look around my world, and not just float in it. Time to grow up. Time to become aware. This explosion is definitely my wake-up call.

The bomb—yes, a bomb—took out the front part of our five-bedroom split level home and the luxurious black limousine that had come to pick up my dad. The limo driver, Jerry, seemed very nice. I only remember meeting him once. I know he was single with no siblings and with just a Mom and Dad who would morn him. Me, I have lots of family. I am not sure what to do. My heart hurts to think about what his parents are going through. I can't imagine losing mom and dad. My parents called his parents. That seemed right. Catholic kids are taught at a young age to pray and let God take over. So, I did. That didn't't make me feel better but it is all I have.

Our house is what's called a split level. Think four big boxes sitting on each other but staggered, kind of like steps. You have to walk up to the front door, which is between level one and level two. The front door is a shiny black solid oak barrier to the world. This design makes my room over part of the garage. I know this sounds complicated but it's really not. The rolling landscape and small hills make this house design popular.

I heard the goodbyes as my Dad and Sean walk out to the limo but return when Mom calls, "Whitey, come back for a minute and see Lucy's science project." Mom yells at me to say goodbye to Dad and I did from my room, under the covers. I am being lazy.

I guess Lucy has hauled her erupting volcano out. She just wants Dad to see it. His attention is important to her. I understand how she feels. I like his attention too. I like Moms attention too, and it is easier to come by. But my sister is primarily interested in Dads attentiveness. I don't interfere, it's not smart to get between Lucy and Dad when she wants his attention.

I can hear Lucy ask, "What do you think, Dad? Is it ok?" Our parents will be out of the country starting the next day, so Lucy is taking advantage of this attention before they both leave.

Dad and Sean ask in unison. "Does it work?" I never heard Lucy's answer because of the blast. BOOM. It was crazy. The air in the room left, then came back in a rush with everything around me is moving, including me. Just like that it is over.

The large cedar tree blocks the view of the limo and driver from the front door where Mom, Dad, Sean and Lucy were standing. The explosion would have killed my dad and Sean if they had not come back to the front door.

Thank God, I was being lazy and still under the warm cozy covers cause when the windows blew out, the glass went everywhere in my room. I was blown off the bed and onto the floor, between the bed and the dresser rapped mostly in my comforter. That drop to the floor and the bedclothes kept me from most of the glass and debris.

My room is directly over the garage doors and the Limo was

right below and about ten feet from the house. There is glass sticking out of everything, including me. Some are embedded in my neck, and my hair and in my bed clothes. As I look around, I can see some big pieces in the far wall by the dresser and my beautiful, blue, canopy bed drapes above me are shredded.

What a noise. What a mess. What the heck just happened? Did Lucy's volcano malfunction?

A heartbeat later, I take an inventory of myself. Self, am I alive?I think so. I decide to move my body parts slowly. Everything seems to work without too much pain. Yep, I am still alive. But Yikes! Warm, wet weird. I slowly drag my fingers across my cheek.

Wow. Damn. Uhhh darn. Oh Hell No. That hurts. The sharp pain is now in my fingers too. It is glass, and I am bloody. Crap, it's mine. Okay, I need help. I am not good with *any* blood and *this* blood is mine. I close my eyes tight and hope this is a bad dream. But, it's not I think. When I open my eyes again, I look up and an angel appears. You know, like in the Christmas story, "And, an Angel appeared in the heavens, and there is radiant light." except my parents are standing there next to this angel. Why are my parents intruding on my dream, in this lovely moment?

The radiant light is actually where the front wall of my bedroom used to be, but now it's gone. Yes, gone and there are lots of lights, red and blue, bouncing around my room. My angel is talking to me. Why can't I hear him? Dad and Mom are talking too. Okay, I'm deaf but alive this angel is tall, has curly blondish, thick hair, deep blue eyes, and he is looking intently into my eyes. I look back and smile. His smile changes. He looks worried. What am I doing wrong?

Okay, I see it now. He has a uniform on. I realize he is a paramedic guy, such a letdown. I thought my time had come, and an angel really had appeared.

I guess I must have passed out for a while because all hell had broken loose. The next thing I know I am loaded onto a gurney and strapped down. I know I need medical help, but how are these paramedics going to get this gurney through the narrow hall, down four steps, make a hairpin turn to the dining room, through the kitchen and probably a debris pile, then down four more steps to the destroyed front door. I give them credit, they tried and tried. They even set the gurney on its end to try to get around the turns, but no luck.

It is so confusing when your hearing isn't working. After a couple attempts and it looked like some harsh words to each other about getting the gurney through the door, I'm lowered to the waiting firemen through the hole in the wall in my room. Crazy, right? I knew it should be loud because there were police cars and firetrucks and ambulances and with lots of people standing or running around, all talking and moving quickly. But it wasn't. My ears just didn't't work. What feels like seconds after I'm lowered from my room, the ambulance is moving, I am on my way to the hospital. When we arrive, I realize the hospital is worse, and it's crazier, too.

TWO

LANGLEY OPS

- Emergency change in security.
- I need everyone listening to your new assignments.
- We had two operatives and their family, and their security detail almost taken out this morning.
- One of the security team, Jerry Williams was killed.
- Both operatives, Whitey and Big Bird have surface injuries.
- Their girls also have minor injuries.
- Sean Mac Elroy, their bodyguard has surface injuries.
- Emergency agents were sent to the hospital.
- Big Bird and Whitey will be on their way to their current assignment a day late, which shouldn't compromise their cover
- The two girls, Tiger and Kitten, will be taken to a secure boarding school in Frederick, Maryland.
- The Media has been handled.You have your assignment packets. Go over them and move out.
- There is not much intel on who and why, except current ops. We will have more soon.
- Check in often and stay updated. Things are changing quickly.
- Situation is fluid.

THREE

The Hospital

MOM AND LUCY ARE THERE in the ER area too. I can see Mom and Dad talking to Lucy. All of us are bloody, even, Dad. Lucy has a bloody nose, and so does Mom. It looks like they did not get much glass in them. I guess the huge cedar tree, the plexiglass screen door and the heavy oak front door shielded them. My canopy bed and covers didn't do as well for me. People, well medical people, keep getting in my face and talking. I think they are talking. I can't hear anything, except buzzing. I point to my ears; nurses look in them and frown.

So, I decide to mouth the words, I can't hear. Finally, a nurse, a cute male one, starts to tell others. "She must not be able to hear."

He takes a piece of paper and writes, "Can't hear?", I smile and nod.

He then writes, "Can't talk either?"

Stupid me, I guess I can talk. I guess I had not made a sound. Why am I mouthing the words? So, I answer by talking. I think my volume is off because everyone stops what they are doing and looks at me.

The cute nurse writes "I think that is a little too loud but keep talking to us".

It's hard to talk and not hear yourself but I try.

Finally, I am in my hospital room. I think it's the first night, everything is such a blur. Where is everyone. I don't like being alone and not know why we were the targets of the bomb, who is out there that wants us dead? This crazy day started early and has gone on forever. My mind is fuzzy. I have a bandage around my neck and both arms. They only hurt a little. I remember Mom and Dad telling me they would be back in a week and not to worry. Nothing new there, they were always traveling on business. Maybe I should be sad that they are not here but, I'm not this is normal. I love them and I know they love me and they will be back, I think. After today I will worry.

When the nurses aren't checking on me and taking blood pressure readings, my day is mostly spent sleeping. I have a dream that is so real, it scares me, and it excites me. You know the kind that is so lovely and sensuous but naughty and delicious! I read about this kind of adventure in some of the magazines I get. In this dream another gorgeous man is hovering over me at my bedside. Not the paramedic, or the nurse, or Sean. So, I am trying to focus. Can there be that many beautiful men, in uniform, in one place? Who knew a hospital could be filled with them? I thought that was only on military bases.

He is a tall, Mediterranean looking man, with dark brown, longish hair that frames his face in soft curls. His face is just barely peeking out of his hoodie. I want to push it off his shadowed face, but my arms are too heavy. My limbs just won't cooperate. The muscles in his neck flex as he leans into me. His cologne just oozes sexual emotions from me. I want to bury my face in his neck so I can breathe him in. I have read in magazines that when you do that, it is quite an exhilarating experience. I am startled when he kisses me on the forehead. I want his lips on mine. I want to remember this dream forever.

He leans close again. Ok kiss me again, this time hit the lips. I can only hope. But no he has flowers, wait, Gardenias I just love the smell of them. I would have really liked the kiss, but Gardenias are my favorite. Last time I remember having Gardenias was in Puerto Rico when we lived there. I was five. We lived way up on a hill on base, Roosevelt Roads. They grew out in front of our home. I would pick one every day. I want to talk with my midnight visitor, but the pain meds make it hard to concentrate and my voice just doesn't want to work. All I can get out is "my favorites". I kind of point at the Gardenias with my eyes.

He comes in close and kisses me on the forehead again and smiles "I know, kitten."

I smile.

I'll see you soon."

I close my drug-induced eyes to sleep. Wait. Kitten? How does he know my nickname! The one Sean gave me? Did Sean tell everyone his name for me? Hmmm, I'll ask him. I thought that was our secret. This visit should have not only scared me but really frightened me but it didn't't. There is a noise by the door. This dream is so real. Where is he going? That's not the exit. That's the bathroom. I am thinking delicious things about him. I drift away.

Seconds later, well, who knows how long, the nurse wants my blood pressure, again. I am already tired of this blood pressure thing. I can't imagine how people who are here a long time endure this intrusion. I want my dream back. I look all around for my visitor, half-hoping it was not a dream. It seemed so real. I think I can even still smell the Gardenias.

The thing is after the nurse leaves, Sean arrives. The Gardenia smell is still there. Sean has a small bandage on the side of his face. He seems to be alright, but he does look tired. He starts by telling me Mom and Dad are on their way to their jobs and Okay. There are clothes for me in the bag in the closet. Lucy and I will be leaving in a couple hours, so get ready. I'm stunned I can kind of hear him though the buzzing.

"Can you say that again because I think I really heard you." It's amazing. I'm starting to hear again. Then he repeats his news. "Kitten, You will be leaving here in an hour or so." He turns to leave.

"Hey wait, did you tell anyone you call me Kitten?" I have sat up and plan to grab him and get an answer, but he turns back.

His brows scrunch together, "What?" He fidgets for a moment.

Is he feeling guilty? No that is worry on his face.

"Why ask me that?"

I just stare, I'm really confused.

Resigned he continues. "That's your call name."

Surprised and baffled, I ask, "What's a call name?"

"Well it's what we use instead of your real name. Lucy is tiger, your dad is Whitey, and your mom is Big Bird, and don't ask why we call her Big Bird, and you are Kitten. So, people who know your parents, know your call name. Why?"

I close my eyes to think. Before I can ask, "Why not Emmy? It's my name. It seems simpler." I realize I'm starring past him at the gardenia plant on the table. I can't breathe. I just stare at it. He's speaking but I am not even listening. Then he steps in front of me.

"You are not listening. What are you looking at?" He follows my line of sight and turns to look at the teddy bear from our neighbors that I sit for and the gardenias. "Where did these come from?"

I tell him about the teddy bear and the neighbors.

He holds up his hand before I can finish and says, "I mean the flowers."

So, I tell him about my dream. I leave out the part about how my midnight visitors cologne made me feel but I did tell Sean, my dream guy had on mémorable Cologne. My dad always says, "Tell me all you know, not just what you think I want to hear." It's a game we play in a crowd. His words come to me, "Observe. Remember. Calculate where you are and how to leave if you need to, and why." I love playing that game. Mom plays sometimes too. So, I even tell Sean about Mr. Dream guy not going out the door but into the bathroom instead.

To my surprise, he pulls his gun, backs to the door, to get help. He makes a tactical move to the bathroom door with the other guy. A few tense moments later, it is cleared, and he returns to me.

He finds gloves in the medical supplies near my bed, then picks up the plant without touching the pot and the bear, and takes them away. He acts like they're contagious or poisonous.

Gosh, I liked my presents, I want both back.

When he returns without them, I start to tell him, "I want to keep them."

He holds his hand up, "Is there anything else I should know?"

The other two guys who came with him are looking all over the room. They are running their hands under surfaces and behind drapes. So weird.

He asks again, "Is there anything else I should know?"

"Oh, Uhh.no, well he leaned over and kissed my forehead. That's when I smelled his cologne. Is that important?"

I start to touch my forehead to show him where he kissed me when Sean snatches up my hand so fast you would think he has superpowers. "Don't touch that." I shrink back and say, "Okaaaayyy."

Sean goes over to the door and back in a flash. Sean, my personal superhero, returns with a swab and attacks my forehead. I raise my hands to protest. He stops and looks at me sideways but continues on. I lower my hands in surrender. "So the midnight visitor is not part of the hospital?"

Sean turns and walks towards the door. "Hey Sean do you hear me?"

He just keeps walking. Over his shoulder he says. "Get ready to leave."

I can tell this visitor is trouble by the odd conversations that Sean has at the door and of course his stern voice. More than a little trouble, I think.

FOUR

LANGLEY OPS

- OK, team here's your update. The bomb was pretty generic device.
- Lab so far has found nothing noteworthy about it. Details are in your notes. If you see some anomaly speak up.
- Lab work on items in kitten's hospital room discovered a small tracking device attached to the bear. Nothing on the plant. We have shared intel with Interpol for any help they can give.
- Description of the suspect is in your packet on the table, including a fuzzy photo from security camera as he enters thehospital. This lead we have from the hospital is being developed as we speak.
- No fingerprints or enough DNA were collected. That intel is in your packet. Vet anyone who fits it.
- Both girls are safe. Big Bird and Whitey are on the ground in South America.
- For now, we think we have a good plan in place.
- Keep your eyes open and vet anyone and everyone new who comes near the two girls.
- Both parents requested the same thing before they left, just keep them safe.

FIVE

Boarding School

THE BOMB WAS A TIMED devise and it could have detonated anywhere and anytime. Lucky the Limo was sitting in our driveway otherwise it could have caused much more devastation and deaths had it been on the road. It is so scary to think about that. Dad told us that the neighbors will be scared too if they know it was a bomb. So we should say it was the water heater that exploded. He is like that always thinking of other's feelings. Isn't that lying is all I can think about. Mom said it isn't a lie if it is to just keep peace and we know the truth. We all agree, it is best to keep the peace and so the story went, the water heater exploded. Can a water heater explode, and can it do that much damage? I wonder.

I never lived there again, they packed us up and we moved. I knew right then and there something was different in my life but it just sat in the back of my mind waiting for me to figure it out. Do I really want to know? That lovely gardenia and Teddy bear I received were never seen again but I will always remember my gardenias. Those gardenias were my first flowers, I mean given to me only. Okay that's scary. My midnight visitor reminds me of the models you see in the magazines, he was tall, tanned, dark hair, very Italian or Mediterranean - looking, quite handsome. The memory of him bending over me keeps swimming around in my head, so elusive. Sean continues to ask me a thousand questions on the way to the new school about my so-called midnight visitor. I tell him everything I can remember over and over. Well, almost, maybe not *every* emotion. That Is mine to keep.He tells me no male nurses logged into my room. Only female nurses, the last was at one o'clock AM to check my blood pressure. The guard at my door was instructed to let only medical personnel in. And, only females logged in according to the my chart. I was only half awake when any came in so I just don't know.

I whip my head around and slowly advise Sean. "My midnight visitor was *definitely* male. I do know the difference." Sean smiles and I think he is not only agreeing that I know the difference but can tell I *like* the difference a lot. Why is he smiling at me so knowingly? I blush. I am so tired of answering the same questions.

As we ride along I-70 West, I am looking at Sean, and daydreaming about him. The beautiful fall scenery is lost to me. We are slowly climbing the rolling hills towards western Maryland but I am not even noticing the blast of fall leaves as we ride. All I can think about is Sean, well maybe beautiful men. Wouldn't it be nice if I was older? He is so fun to look at and be with. I wish he saw me as a *woman* not a little girl. Fat chance. I know in my head I'm not the little girl he sees me as, but I guess I need to act and talk like one in order for him to change his perception of me. I wonder if he has a girlfriend? My midnight visitor was very sexy but Sean is much better than my midnight visitor by a mile, well, in an old-fashioned kind of way. Sean is a take charge get it done right kind of guy who makes all my girl parts want him to take charge and get it done.

"Kitten, are you listening?"

"Sorry." I look at Lucy, and the long car ride is too much for her-she is asleep in the seat next to me. She is thirteen months younger than me. At that moment, she looks so much younger than that. "Sorry. Sean, I zoned out."

He looks mad, then he sighs and smiles.

The explosion caused my sister Lucy and I to be at boarding school at the Frederick Academy of the Visitation, FAV. If someone would have said Emerald Mist McCormick AKA "Emmy" will be enrolled in a boarding school, I would have laughed my pants off. I mean, I have parents who like me, and our family functions just fine. Why would I need to be somewhere else? But, here I am.

"Sorry Kitten, I am pressing too hard. We'll talk later. Hey Kevin, how much longer?"

Kevin's reply came from the front of the limo. "Turning in at the first gate. We have a security check here, then we are done." Our arrival is mid-morning on a school day. We pass through the back gates, next to the delivery trucks. We are inside one gate and in a courtyard with two delivery trucks next to us. Sean is out the door and in someone's face yelling about security when a plump nun steps around the corner of the inner fence.

Sean's words come out as rapid-fire. "Sister Baptista, this is not the kind of security I expected. I expected more. I expected better." She smiles at Sean and waves our limo through the gate. It closes the old world out, and this new world is stunning. They walk and talk. Sean seems to calm down and smile, so I think all is well. I am a little skittish.

If you have read the book "The Secret Garden", *this* is the place she describes. Everything blooming and green and happy feeling. Three girls ride by on ponies. Yep, ponies. I am dumb founded. Not even one of the girls gave the limo a second look. I always look at limos even though I am in and out of one on a frequent basis. These girls seemed to not notice anything different in this dream-like world around us. I can hear singing somewhere in the distance that feels like a church choir, sort of heavenly. I can also hear girls talking and giggling just past a small maze of bushes. Sean is deep in conversation with Sister Baptista and the driver is unloading out suitcases on to a trolly for transport somewhere.

Lucy who I thought was sound asleep has come alive and dashes out the door trying to catch up with the girls on ponies. She does catch them, and after a few nods and a wave to them, she strides back with a smile on her face. I knew then she will be A-Okay here.

The Frederick Academy of the Visitation is different. Okay I have been in schools that have walls all around them and tight security. But not in the US. The Frederick Academy of the Visitation, FAV for short is in the heart of Frederick Maryland. Sean handed us both over to Sister Baptista and Sister Mary Catherine. Our unloaded luggage has disappeared already. Sean

hugs us both. and Sean and Kevin depart. I will miss seeing Sean every day. The next days are busy with learning where things are and which uniform to wear and when. I screw that up a lot.SIX
Langley OPS

Security check at the back gate of the girl's school seems inadequate according to Sean Mac Elroy. A team has been dispatched to evaluate it. There are more assets there that need the same security as the girls if it is a weakness that can't continue. I will apprise you when those changes occur, and we will check again.

There are two other teams being dispatched to check other nearby facilities where we have assets.

Check your asset assignments. I want a full report on all possible weakness in twenty-four hours.

SIX

Frederick Academy of the Visitation

———

MY SISTER SHOULD BE IN the seventh grade, but because of her test scores, she must do the sixth grade again. I will begin the eighth grade here. She resents having to do sixth grade again, a lot. I understand her feelings, but I am glad it is not me. I think this is good because her new friends here won't be any the wiser about her past unless she tells them. The class sizes are small here. I have eight girls in my eighth grade, and she has seven in her class. And here, this year I learn more than curriculum. For the most part. I will not miss FAV. But here is where I begin to learn how to be friends with girls that are my age - seriously scary task.

In the past, when we went to gatherings where there would be other kids my age I would run and hide in plain sight. This worked best in a crowd of adults standing around talking especially the tall ones, sort of like hiding in a forest. Most often, I would seek out the younger kids, you know the "curtain crawlers" and become overly animated with them and their toys just to steer clear from the other females my age in the room. Other parents would notice me, and I guess think I just loved little kids and smile at me. These Mom's would say "You are good with kids" and "You could be a good teacher and great Mom". I do like little kids but they are also great camouflage too.

And, I always have a book with me. Reading is one of my favorite things to do to while hiding. Finding a quiet place to read took the covert skill, I have acquired. Whether I am at a social gathering or this new school, I try to find a secluded place for a mental break. One of these three plans of escape from other teenage girls usually work. I don't know why, but girls my age are so scary. I think it is because they lie and manipulate, gossip and are just weird.

Okay so, boys might be that scary too but they don't count cause I don't get close to them either. And, if they are interested in me, I haven't noticed any. I wonder if I am like these other girls, and just don't know I am. God, I hope not. Being imprisoned at the FAV with 171 girls ages five to fourteen is terrifying. It makes me want to hide out. So, I become super-aware of hiding places just to be alone.

I make it my priority to find some places for me to just be alone. I am not afraid to talk to people. It's just that teenage girls are difficult and teenage boys, well, I don't know, how I am with teenage boys yet. Time will tell. I am always around adults. In the first four days, I find five really good, quiet places and three so-so ones. From the nook above the door to the theater just big enough for me to curl into and read a book, to the small closet in the gym that hasn't seen a human in years, I have eight escape places. I have to clean the closet in the gym just to be in it. So much dust and spiders. Yikes

To my surprise, one afternoon, I find Caroline Anderson in my quiet favorite place. My first thoughts are why is she here? why is she following me around? and how do I get rid of her quietly? I know who she is, but I haven't really talked to her. She is an eighth grader like me and lives in the bed chamber next to mine. We have three-sided bed chambers with a sliding door on the fourth wall in each bed chamber. There is a twin bed, a closet, a desk and a chair in each one. I don't know why it is called a chamber because it is just a bedroom but who knows. These nuns have weird names for everything. Bed chamber sounds so Medieval. The space is small, but it works. And it is easy to keep everything in order.

She has never spoken to me, but I have watched her try to blend into the wall in a room whenever there are more than two people in a space. She really has nothing to worry about, this place does not *force* you to be social. Of course. she looks like the original Barbie doll that everyone wants to be or wants to be around. And, she is a desired classmate and friend, just not mine? The really pretty girls that are so put together scare me the most. She is that girl, and she is super scary. I wonder if she knows how scary she really is.

One afternoon, as I crawl in backwards to my very special hidey hole. My butt bumps into something. It is Caroline, she sort of squeaks. I have practiced control, so I just glare and keep my noise inside. We both freeze. I whirl around hitting my head on the keyboard above us. We are in the balcony of the chapel under the foot petals of the huge organ.

I want to escape, or better yet, just vanish. I can see myself in her, I can see her fear. We will have to speak. A major challenge for me. Looking into her deep blue eyes I can see it is true for her too. For just a second, I feel the pull of her life force on me.

Then I am blinded by a huge light. This flashlight makes me reach out grab it and shove it in my pocket. Is she crazy? I really wanted to hit her with it so she would never do that again, but I didn't't. Caroline is clearly not remembering where we are. Under the foot petals of the big organ in the chapel is not like walking through a forest at night. This is serious punishment for being here without permission. The lights are all out right now except the candles by the alter. This human yelped and I push forward clasping my hand across her mouth. She bit me, I yelped. At this noise the lights go on in the chapel.

"Who's there?"

We freeze. Sister Mary Catherine comes into view carrying her dust mop and peering around the chapel. "

I know someone's in here. Come out and show yourself."

Thank God, she did not look up. I don't think this very petite nun with her thick coke bottle glasses can see more than ten feet ahead of her. At least, I hope not. I feel exposed, angry with Caroline for intruding in my space. I stay as flat as I can and try to stop breathing. Caroline seems to be frozen too. Caroline's face is now so close we could have kissed. I want to move. I need space. I blink, she blinks. I swallow, she swallows. This is more than awkward. Thank God again, that it is just our faces that are so close. I have listened to the teasing Caroline has endured about whether she likes girls or boys or both. I don't know-or care-as long as she keeps her distance from me. Not easy at the moment.

It is so mean what the girls say to her, about her, against her. I know I like boys. But, what about her? God, I hope she likes boys and not girls. I am praying a lot lately. At least I am in church. Correction in the chapel that is nestled between the school and the convent. If she gets any closer, I will have to make her move away and it will be noisy. Then, we will be found. The clock ticks on and on and on. I can hear Sister Mary Catherine moving around down below us. I hear the bells start ringing in the distance, they are the clanging for evening prayers in the convent.

Sister Mary Catherine's shoes start a quick tapping across the chapels, lovely tile floor away from us. Then all the lights go on in the whole chapel in preparation for evening prayers, not just the chapel floor area but the balcony where we are too. Then the slow thunderous closing of the large wooden door that goes into the convent. Sister Mary Catherine will be back in minutes with the rest of the convent for evening prayers. I don't want to be here when Sister Clair comes in to play the organ.

Caroline's head pops up and she begins to move. Caroline is up and moving so fast in the wrong way. She heads towards the convent door just past the end of the organ, and I grab at her.

Whispering aloud," Where do you think you are going?"

She gives me the "be quiet" signal. "

Come on, it's safe this way." Really? I'm not sure but without a plan of my own I follow.

There, behind the organ, is a small cabinet door that I hadn't noticed before. She opens it and crawls in. I hesitate, then I hear the doors opening on the chapel floor and the balcony. I hear that familiar sound of the nuns shuffling in for prayers. I hear the murmur of low voices. They have begun their prayers. It would be seconds before Sister Clair arrives to play the organ. I scramble in without a thought to where I am going.

This is like Alice following the rabbit down his rabbit hole. My leap of faith has me popping out in the dark infirmary next to a file cabinet. Thank God! we have escaped, and we giggle at each other. I then, stop dead still and realize she is-or could be-a friend.

We scramble out of the infirmary and onto the big porch that runs around the perimeter of the buildings that face the stunning gardens watching the nuns just closing the chapels door. We sit for a moment with our backs against the building wall and just breath. Scary and exciting all in one. The sun is just sinking below the trees and a chilly breeze moves our hair. Safe for now. This is an interesting beginning to a what would become a fabulous friendship.

I soon learn Caroline is the best kind of friend you can have. In my head I am secure with what I like and don't with other kids and I get lost in those relationships. Caroline is different, she helps me realize you can be unsure on the inside but strong on the outside. I like this inner confidence she is teaching me. She helps me realize my dreams will not happen if I just sit back and watch. I enjoy the "Kirby Scott Show" and dream about dancing on it. Caroline likes to dance, but she is so much better at drawing. I encourage her to enter art contests, and she makes me realize if I want to dance, I will have to step up and do something out of character. So, I do I write to the show, asking what do I need to do in order to get to dance on their show. Mentally, I cross my fingers for a chance at this.

SEVEN

To Dance

I KNOW THE BOMBING CHANGED ME. I just feel different about my world. I find myself looking closely at everything and everybody in a suspicious way. My sister's view of safety changed too. She wants to learn to shoot a gun. When we are home, or with Mom's brothers, she asks to be included in learning about hunting with rifles at our family hunting camp in western Maryland. She is granted this support and I follow and learn too. I am sure this self-defense is a good idea for me as well. Missing that secure feeling of safety at St Mary's Catholic School in Hagerstown left Lucy and me rethinking what safety is a lot. Both of us choose to get better prepared.

When Lucy asks Dad, "Why we aren't safe anymore?" he just says, "It is what it is. The world is a changing place. Mom and I are here to take care of that. You only need to be careful." Not only did the bomb change my home and school, but just going places became impossible. I miss that freedom. The freedom of just getting on a bike and feeling the wind in my hair. Freedom lost.

FAV is a beautiful place twelve acres of building and beautiful gardens. I am glad I am having this experience, but I am not really happy here. Yes, I have Caroline as a friend, and the teachers are just fine, and there is always something to do, but I miss my home with family and friends. Lucy thinks I am always competing with her and I hate that feeling. Lis so sure I am always trying to upstage her. But I am not. Truth be told, unless she confronts me it doesn't't back cross my mind. I am so into my own world I don't notice her. I guess that is the problem. I am not a very good big sister. I just know, or think I know, she needs her space. So, I went my own way alone. Well, truth be told, I like being alone. And, now, I have Caroline. Her friendship is the best.

Alone, there are lots of things I can do and be content. Dancing, whether in a crowd or alone, you can disappear in your heart and just exist. I love to dance. I watch "American Bandstand" and "The Kirby Scott Show" any time I can. "The Kirby Scott Show" is a dance show much like "American Bandstand". You know, with Dick Clark out of Philadelphia, but it is the local one out of Baltimore, WBAL. I learn from the "American Bandstand" response to my letter you have to dance at least one season on a local dance show before you can dance with them, and you must be enrolled in high school. I start with "The Kirby Scott Show". Everyone can go to the local show and dance on Friday afternoons, but if you are really good, you can be a regular and can dance on the white pedestals. And, I am good enough. Well, I think I am.

And, if you dance on "The Kirby Scott Show", you can audition for "American Bandstand" or "Soul Train". These two are nationally syndicated dance shows. I dream of dancing on "American Bandstand" And to me that will make me someone special. I am not so sure about "Soul Train". I like the Motown sounds. Really, I like it better than, or at least as much as the Beatles. "The Kirby Scott Show" is the first integrated show of its kind, and I know I need to set my goals on it first. I can hear Caroline in my head say, "If you want it then go get it." I feel brave because of her. Time to plant the seed with my parents.

When my parents are home, I often see them curled up on the love seat in the den talking. This is their favorite place to meet, mostly late, at night when the house is quiet. I don't ask too many questions about what my parents do and don't do. Instead, I listen. Just like any other nosey kid, I try hard to watch and listen. Sitting on the stairs, just out of their sight, is one of my favorite past-times when Lucy and I are home for the weekend from our Catholic boarding school. It helps me figure out where Mom and

Dad are off to next.

It's early 1966. Mom and Dad are talking a lot about the first Jewish baby being born in Spain since 1492. That just sounds crazy. No Jewish kids in Spain? Mom says it makes sense because the Nazi's used Spain as one of their temporary hiding place on their way to South America. She thinks this will bring the last of the Nazi supporters, who had been silent for years, out into the public eye. Gosh, are they going to protest about a baby because he is Jewish? I mean, people are protesting about almost anything and everything these days. But a baby?

I come back from my daydreams to hear Dad say he thinks a trip to Spain is in order. Then they will be on to Paraguay since they are invited to some big party given by someone named Stroessner. Mom is sure this will help them find some Nazi guy who is on the loose. This Stroessner guy is very anti-communist according to Mom, but Dad said he is very dangerous but a necessary evil. Dad and Mom are interested in Martin Luther King as he begins his civil rights campaign. They talk about how he will change things, and they hope for the better. I think they are right. So much anger there and stuff to think about, my head hurts.

My sister needs to learn how to just listen. She is constantly sticking her foot in her mouth. Lucy is thirteen months younger than I am. When she began her life, she was very ill. So, she is very pampered. She will tell you I am the pampered one. I may be spoiled, but she is pampered and spoiled too and so much more. She whines and complains, about things being unequal and not being fair about every little thing she can think of. I feel it is best to just watch and take note. Wait and listen.

So, when Dad said yes he will let me audition for "The Kirby Scott Show well, WOW,"Yes." It is unbelievable. Caroline is right. She said, "If you want something go get it, It is not coming to you." My Dad *never* says yes. He might say "let's talk about it", "let me think about it," or "maybe," or "I doubt that will work" but never just Yes.

I think Mom and Dad know how unhappy and uncomfortable I am at this boarding school. They see Lucy is doing well in school and socially, so she is in the right place. But me? Not so much.

I am glad they get it and I love them all the more for that. This opportunity to dance is such a big deal for me. Mom delegated the job of going with me to Dad. Lucky him.

EIGHT

LANGLEY OPS

- Team, listen up.
- We are splitting up our security team on the girls and adding a few for this outing.
- Kitten has a new interest, Whitey and Big Bird want her to have this experience. They are doing their best to keep the girls in as normal environment as possible.
- The advance team will arrive early to secure the TV station. The station manager and his security are aware, on board and have been vetted.
- You have your assignments.

NINE

Dance

"THE KIRBY SCOTT SHOW" IS not a place my dad would *choose* to go, but he does. Amazing for me. My conservative parents take us most everywhere with them. This means from the local restaurants, to a fancy dinner party at some political function, even to a White House event. They always seem comfortable anywhere they go which makes me feel the same. I am surprised my dad is willing to step out of his comfort zone. But he does, and I love him for that. I hear him talk to someone on the phone making arrangements to take me, so yeah, it's happening.

We, my dad, and Sean, and me, walk into WBAL Baltimore. The place is so cool. Everyone is busy and seem, seemingly on a mission. I realize that this conservative sheltered girl has found her kind of place. I could live here and be happy. I have always been the observer, but, thanks to Caroline and her advice I have stepped up to take charge of what I want. So, here it goes. Time to see if I am good enough. I realize the large group of teens over on the left side of the lobby are where I think I need to be. Before I can walk over to them, Sean steps ahead and asks the lady behind the counter for me. She looks up quickly, then waves us forward and through a different door. Guess those other kids still have paperwork to do.

I have never thought so much about my dad and the people around him as I did that day. I am startled in to noticing how other people react around him. The main anchor guy, Rolf Hertsgaard, on the evening news at WBAL, came up to Dad and introduces himself and the others to us. I know this is the guy my parents listen to all the time. Dad shakes his hand and smiles. My dad is quiet, concise, well spoken - a man of few words. Dad is very tall for his generation, lean, blonde, and blue-eyed. He is part-German and looks like what I would think of as an "aryan".

I am not sure I actually heard him speak that day. I am sure he did. But people were talking to him, then nodding and scurrying off. He isn't fazed by all the attention. You would have thought he was the evening anchor. Sean just stands nearby, and watching everything and everyone, just like always.

It is now or never, soooo I decide I need to focus on dancing and not on Dad. I think about how people are reacting to him later. No one said anything to me other than to get me in my dance number. Dad doesn't't seem concerned. Sean just stays close to Dad, especially when the place fills up with lots of people. I did notice some of the kids giving me sideways looks, but I am too nervous to even feel it is important.

My dance number is six, and it is one of my favorite lucky numbers. I focused on dancing and after a while, Dad and Sean fade into the background. It paid off I manage to be in the semi final group. As semi-finalists we are herded into a holding room to wait. Now, I know just how cattle feel when headed to auction. I saw Sean check with the lady in charge of us, but that is normal for him. No worries, I smile and wave, and he waves back with a thumbs up to me.

There are fifty of us and everyone looks so put together. All of a sudden, I feel self-conscience. I am wearing a pair of navy blue dress shorts with matching short-sleeved jacket, a white fitted blouse underneath. I have a large, red, floppy bow just under the peter pan collar. I chose it because I have seen the popular model, Twiggy, wear a similar outfit. I have a red head band on to keep my long straight hair out of my face while I dance. I know I have nice clothes on, and am well groomed. But I am still nervous about how I look. I am fashion conscience, but there is a worldly aura the others seem to be surrounded with. I don't think I have that. I wear a uniform every day at school, so I guess I am not as comfortable in other clothes Some of the kids know each other, and I find by listening to them that they have been here before and are trying out again. I hoped that I will not have to do that because I am pretty sure Dad will not do this again.

As we are about to compete, doing one last dance to find out who made it, I am worried. Suddenly, I am scared and nervous a and I guess it shows on my face. Sean caught my eye. He comes strolling towards me. He is six-foot-something and just amazing looking for a twenty-plus. I think he is twenty-six. Old. My friends think he is more than amazing-they think that he is perfect. Well, I guess he is I saw him once in a swimsuit, and he looked like one of the models in my "Sixteen" magazines. If he gets too close to me and I can smell his alluring cologne, I always struggle to control of my voice.

Sean has sandy blonde hair with touch of red highlights. He has a rugged look but polished too. He looks good in a suit or really anything or maybe nothing. I feel my cheeks redden. I like Sean even though he is twelve years older than me. It is safe to say I have a crush on him.

As he comes close. I feel the butterflies moving in my stomach. If he touches me, I will blush again. Nope. I am already blushing.

Crap. All of the kids around me are watching him. "Okay, Emmy hold on to yourself". Oh God, he looks worried. I wonder what is wrong. Hmmm, come to find out, it is me he is worried about.

He leans in and says quietly in my ear, well really my neck, "What's up, kitten? You look worried."

I look up into his luscious green eyes and blush, then start to sweat. He does that to me.

"Just nervous." Damm did I just squeak?

In one smooth move he bends over and kisses me on the cheek and then breathes into my ear "You got this. Kitten" and then returns to my Dad.

The two girls standing next to me have a not-so-quiet conversation. "Cute bodyguard," says one.

"Wish I had one. I'd at least know what to do with him. This one here is way too young to get it," the second one chirped loudly.

I am mad, and I don't know why. Bodyguard?? Is that what Sean is? I know what to do with him. I have read all about that in the magazines, or at least I think I do. Why are they saying that about me? They don't know me. What makes me look like I don't know what to do. That makes me madder still.I turn to let them have it. I am not sure what I am going to say, but it doesn't't matter. I am angry, very angry just then, the AD (assistant director) calls my name to join the first group. What? Okay, Sure. "

I'm coming." I'll take care of them later. Well here goes nothing. The music began, and I am delighted to hear Honky-tonk Woman, I dance. Then we wait and wait and wait. After what feels like forever, they post the list. I made it. I get to dance.

I think my dad is not too happy, but he says nothing. I kind of think he thought I wouldn't't make it. He smiles at me and gives me a big hug.

"Great job, Emmy."

Sean, however, looks a little worried. What is up with that? The two girls who said they liked Sean also made it. Cookie and Mary Francis, so, I guess I will see more of them later. I will show them who knows how to handle Sean.

I am ready to take care of those two rude females. I have learned how to handle girls like them from Caroline at boarding school. Caroline will be proud of me for my "go get what I want" attitude.

Before I can do anything, Cookie and Mary Francis run up and hug me. In unison, they squeal,»You are such a good dancer. We are going to have so much fun together."

What is happening? Cookie and Mary Francis are trying to be very nice. I like it that they take me under their wing. In the back of my brain I guess I will wonder if it is to get close to Sean or that they just want to be my friend. Time will tell. I will ask Caroline what she thinks. They both go to Catholic High schools on the south side of Baltimore in a place called Glen Burnie. Dad informs me that area is a working man's neighborhood. Does that mean there are neighborhoods where you don't work? How silly that sounds to me.

Sean wants the girls, full names. Does he want to get to know them? Nah, my Mom probably wants to call their mom's since we will be spending many hours together.

Cookie Matcianio is Italian and has beautiful, dark, wavy hair with magnetic dark brown eyes. Cookie has dark brown hair and a perpetual tan and perfect skin. She lives in a mostly Italian part of Glen Burnie. she has four brothers. She is the baby of the family.

Mary Francis Clannahan is half-Irish and half-Italian and an only child Mary Francis is kind of tall and very lean and has mousey brown hair and hazel eyes but pale skin. Cookie is slightly taller than Mary Francis. I have very long dark auburn hair with sun bleached highlights like my mom. I am 5'8", so a little taller than both of them. So, I guess the mix of different looks is important to this TV show. We all can dance. "The Kirby Scott Show" films in Baltimore on Friday nights. I am so ready to dance.

TEN

Langley OPS

- Kitten's security team for taping will be the same team assigned to the Ocean City detail. Her parents want her to have as normal experience as possible for as long as possible and still be safe.
- Tiger's team is reduced for the time being, she will be at Patuxent Naval Air Base or nearby at the Belvedere Hotel and Resort owned by Big Bird's sister.
- Big Bird's sister is aware of security and will cooperate in any way.
- Again, keep the girls safe while Whitey and Big Bird are on assignment.
- Intel on bomb and bomber is still ongoing with not much new.
- See your packets for details.

ELEVEN

Ocean City

THE SMALL SCARS ON MY neck from the glass embedded by the bomb will hardly be noticeable by the time I began dancing on the show, and any visible marks can be hidden by makeup. I guess the small brown marks on my neck look like freckles but I see them every time I look in the mirror and the memories of that day flood back. The first taping of "The Kirby Scott Show" is three months away. I am glad it will be summer soon and then High school, which means, no Frederick Academy of the Visitation. School will not interfere. I am going to be a freshman this next year and figure we can work out the schedule for the Friday afternoon taping later.

One of the coolest surprises at the end of my eighth grade at the boarding school is a weekend trip to Ocean City, Maryland. It is a tradition and a great one. One of the parents who arranged the trip has a house there and rents it out all the time. I am one of the eight graduating eighth graders. So the girls going are Janet, Carol, Susan, Linda, Sharon, Shelly, Caroline and me, so cool.

We are all invited for the weekend. Our little group was given four bedrooms in this house of twelve suites. A fifth suite has the chaperone who is Mary Anne, Janet's sister. Mary Anne is in college and is accompanied by her friend. Her male friend. This sheltered Catholic girl is stunned. Janet's sister is sleeping with a man; she is happy, pretty, normal, sweet, and there was no big *A* on her back. She is happy to show him off as hers.

I have never met anyone who is unmarried and sleeping together.

It is so enlightening and liberating. Okay, I know, *sheltered* and dumb.

We arrive at the house mid-day on Friday. The eight of us came in two suburban's Mary Anne drove one with Janet, Carol, Susan and Linda. Janet's mom drove the other suburban with Caroline, Sharon, Shelly, and I in it. We are standing in front of a three-story Victorian house. It is bright yellow. You could find this house with your eyes closed. The outside could pass as a lovely Victorian home that is well-kept, except for the color. Walking inside, I feel the beach vibe in this oh-so-typical beach house.

Standing just inside the door, the big lobby area is only dwarfed by the wide stairs that go straight up to the second floor. It could pass for the entrance to a palace with a little renovation. You can see the walkway that circles around all four walls of the second floor with room doors visible through the white railing. The most impressive part of the second floor is the dozen or so stunning male specimens waxing their surf boards. Their boards are spanning the space across the lobby from one Janet's mom driving side-rail to the other. The boys are bare chested and tan, so nice.

Caroline stops dead, I am hoping my mouth is not hanging open. These boys are all AMAZING looking. Then, one of the boys, no men, or really David-like guys, came running down the stairs and straight for Caroline. He picks her up and twirls her around kissing her on the neck. He is talking rapidly at her.

"Hey sis, didn't know you were coming."

I didn't know Caroline had a brother.

"Janet didn't't tell me. How long are you staying?" He stops suddenly, looking over Caroline's shoulder at me. He looks so far into my eyes, I went numb. "Who is this cutie? Your friend, I hope?" Caroline introduces me to Kurt Kennedy, her brother from another mother. We all make plans to go to the beach in thirty minutes, so Caroline and Kurt can catch up.

I have a tough time releasing myself from his intense stare. Or, is it Kurt, who can't let go?

Caroline smiles, tilts her head, and then she takes my hand like I am five and leads me away to our room. The other girls are long gone to their rooms and are already heading to the beach.

    I am rooming with Caroline, and we are on the first floor like all the other girls. Our room is all pastel pinks and greens, so feminine. The large king bed is under the window with a low rose patterned padded headboard. It is really nice. There is a love seat at the end of the bed that immediately becomes our junk pile as we change into swimsuits. Soon we are ready to go. We meet Kurt and two of his friends.

TWELVE

LANGLEY OPS

- Short update on Ocean City detail. Intel has provided info on others at the beach house where kitten is.
- Guest of note is Kurt Kennedy, one of" The Kennedy" clan.
- Kitten detail has a few snags and two agents added and one extracted due to minor injuries in Ocean City MD.
- Tiger detail is good.
- Whitey and Big Bird still out of country.
- They will need background intel on all of the socially active families in the area.
- Tiger detail no change

THIRTEEN

The beach at Ocean City

ALL HAVE SURF BOARDS UNDER their arms, in the lobby. The one-block walk to the boardwalk following these men is eye opening again. I am so aware of their bodies, and that I am with them. Cool.The cool of coolness stopped when Sean and two others walk up to me. This stops our small parade, and everyone stares.

Sean starts right in at me then leans in and whispers in my ear, "Kitten, we'll be close, so no worries. Your Dad says to give you space. We will do our best but it is not our strong suit."

I thank him and encourage everyone to move forward. No one moves. It takes a minute and I blush, and again encourage everyone to move but most just stare at the retreating group.

By the time a place on the beach is selected to set up our umbrella and spread out our beach blanket. I still feel the wondering eyes all over me. I need to learn to get used to this, but what is this? I try to just act normal, so I fish for the baby oil in my bag. I am aware I am alone for the moment. Thank goodness, I need a moment to get my thoughts together. I start to put baby oil on my skin hopping the umbrella will do its job of shielding my fair skin from the intense sun and the stares of everyone else. I burn just looking at the sun, let alone being in it full blast.

Kurt plops down next to me. Okay, here come the questions. I want to look at him but I feel the heat rising in my face, and the sun did not cause it. I wait and wait and wait. Then, well then I feel his hands applying the baby oil on my back. I shiver. He notices. Leaning in he breathes his words down my neck. "Emmy, lie down on your stomach so I can get this even." I am terrified. I so want to do this, but I feel like I am standing on the edge of a cliff, and this cliff jumping is so hard. I obey, willing to do most anything he asks because my brain is not responding. All my girl parts are ruling. I lie down on the towel and get ready to enjoy his hands on my back. He unhooks the back of my bathing suit top and I freeze. His gentle touch rivaled that of a new mom applying baby oil to a newborn baby's butt. Though, I did not feel innocent like a baby. I feel a little naughty, and it is sooooo intriguing. I wonder who is watching. Do I care?

Just at that moment Kurt's hands graze the edge of my swimsuit bottoms. I stifle a moan and cough. I can feel his smile he knows his effect on me. I feel naked. Well, I almost am. My immediate reaction is desire, and he knows it.

But that doesn't't mean he will get what he wants. I am sheltered, and I know it. I desire to be out there enjoying everything but I am also cautious. Okay, okay, okay, brain let me think this through so, I am confused and scared and a new teenager. The silence around us is so weird, kind of like we entered a world of our own, and it is just the two of us. The umbrellas are a lot of the view, but why hasn't Sean intruded like he always does?

Kurt leans over, and just when I think he is going to kiss my neck, he settles down next to me. He is quiet for a long time. I am quiet too, but for me, it is to gain composure and let my brain take control again, not my girl parts. He is so close, our bodies are sort of slippery and next to each other all the way down from arm to hip to thigh. So delightful my body is touching his and I am slippery.

Should I offer to do the same for him? That would be nice, not just for him but for me. I start to sit up when I realize my top is not on me too. Kurt sits up quickly too. We were facing each other. I grab my top in the front and hold it close. He reaches both arms around me, leans in, and reconnects my top for me. This move put us so close and intimate that the kiss is no surprise. It is necessary. My ragged breathing is echoed by his, and the long kiss barely satisfied our desire of the moment. I want more.

Kurt's friends call him; he jumps up, and trots off, looking back once before he hits the water. Our little personal world disappears, and all of the noisy world comes back full blast. Caroline is standing there, talking about eating. I look up and just nod and smile. She has ordered lunch. I wonder what we are having. Turns out it is the ever-popular pizzas, and tasty I think even though I am watching Kurt the whole time I ate. More swimming and napping. I am dreaming, very pleasant thoughts. When I look at the others, I notice most are sleeping or reading, I need a walk.

I get up and set out. I see Sean in the distance, but he does not approach. Kurt catches up and starts talking, asking questions about Sean. Of course, I answer as much as I can about my world. Sean jogs up to us and quietly asked for Kurt's name. Kurt stops dead and I can see his personal wall fall into place. A long pause doesn't even fit as a good description of the time that elapses in silence. I truly thought I felt my hair grow. I hope Sean doesn't ruin this, whatever "this" is.

Sean finally breaks the silence by stepping up close. "This young woman cannot be compromised and to detour that, I must vet her friends, especially *new* friends. You are in that group. I can see she likes you. I want to make it easier for her to keep you as a friend. So, settle down young man, I am not here to mess with you, just protect her."

I look up, and Sean smiles. "Emmy, if this guy is smart, he can see a good thing. He'll understand, it just is what it is." Why am I always so surprised when I hear Sean talk about protecting me? What can be so important that I am being protected from? I can't even look at Kurt. I just what to be normal- fat chance. I try to look through my lashes, watch both men.

Kurt looks back and forth between us, then puts his hand under my chin and lifts it so I can see his eyes and says, "It's Kurt Matthew Kennedy, I should be easy to find since I have high profile family members in politics too." He turns and jogs away.

I turned, put my hands on my hips, and tried to sound indignant, "Well that went well, Sean. How about hanging a sign around my neck that says "untouchable"? And did you catch who he is related to?"

Sean came in very close to my nose, his voice is a low growl. "I don't care who he is related to. He already got too close, and there was a lot of touching, so I think that horse is already out of the barn and running down the street on a wild tear. And according to your dad you are untouchable. Your mom will not approve. Would you care to explain that to your mother, who, by the way, scares me more than your dad."

I take a step back, I need a moment so that I don't squeak out my answer but my voice came out in a strong competent voice. Yeah me. "Okay, I get it. I'll be careful," I turn and continue my walk. I really need to cool off because of both men but in very different ways and for different reasons. Men, my emotions and this teen thing are confusing. God help me.

As this day wore on, I learn more about Kurt. He seems like a good guy, but he can have any girl he wants, including the very popular ones. I usually am not in the popular-group, I fall into a very different category. Caroline is very much the Barbie doll type. When I am with her, I get an up-close look at the very popular and wealthy ones' way of life. Very interesting species. I am not sure I can keep up with this crowd.

We have a lot planned for the next two days, but I know my freedom is short-lived. So, I go dancing with the other girls I came with. I know Sean, or one his crew, is out there watching. Caroline is off to dinner with one of the beautiful boys from upstairs. We, the other girls from school and I dance on the big pier. I am having a great time. I love to dance. We dance the night away.

The other girls seem to have disappeared from the pier without me noticing. Caroline would never have done that. I am dreading the short, two-block walk, back to the house. I am nervous all the way. Head up, Emmy, Sean and his team are in the shadows. It is late when I get back. The doors are locked, I don't have a key. So, I go looking for my window. I can't get in without anyone knowing maybe I can wake up Caroline. Maybe Sean will appear.

The window is open. I feel so lucky, but it is so high, I can't reach it. Even though it is a first-floor room, the building is raised off the ground, so storms don't flood it.

Caroline doesn't't answer to my calls. I turn around and just lean up against the building to think. The cutest little cat is perched on the trash can in the yard next door. I might not have seen this little cutie if she had been black, but she is a bright yellow calico. She stands up and starts to dance around on the lid of the trash can. without much thought I decide to walk over and dance with her. She looks up at me, grabs the bug she is dancing with, and takes off. I am left with the trash can.

The trash can. Okay, I smile, and I am happy to pick up my gift. I take it to just below the window. Instead of dancing on the trash, can I climb in the window.

Well, really, I just fall in. Thank goodness, the bed is there, and Caroline. I did not fall on her, but she stirs and I freeze. I don't want to wake her up because I will have to explain why I had to climb in a window.I change into my nightgown and crawl under the covers. The night is cool and breezy, so I lay there with my eyes shut letting the gentle breeze float across my face. I open my eyes because I hear the trash can move. Is my pretty little yellow kitten doing her dance again. Then, there is a bigger noise, too much for a small cat. Is it a burglar? Or worse.

I am stone still. This large shadow looms over me as it slides in through the window. Way too big for the kitten. He, well, I think it is a "he" that slides into the room and onto the bed. I look at this intruder through my lashes. I don't want him to realize I am awake. I move my hand getting ready to clobber this intruder with the lamp on the bedside table when he belches a yucky beer smell and rolls over towards me, I can see it is a drunk, passed out Kurt. His beautiful face rests next to mine, and he is out cold. He looks like he has a bloody nose and black eye. How did that happen? Where is Sean! How did Kurt get in unnoticed? Somebody will be in trouble, but I really don't care. Kurt is so cute, even when he is drunk. This is fun well, no, this is exciting, well, this is different and scary.

I knew I couldn't't move him. He is out cold, so I try to wake him. He doesn't even flinch when I push at him. I guess I can literally say I have now slept with a man. Not so sure I will sleep, but that is fine with me. I will just enjoy the scenery and hope he doesn't belch again. I do drop off to sleep, only to wake with Kurt's arm draped over my body, and he is spooning up against me. I move a little and then hold my breath as he snuggles closer. His snore is soft, and his steady breathing is lovely. I like being trapped under his arm.

My imagination wanders all different directions about what to say, what will happen next, what will Caroline say. Crap, Caroline. She is here too in bed, technically a threesome. Not so cool, but nothing can be done to change this.

I think he is dreaming because he was mumbling and holding me tighter. This is nice. Then, things changed, my girl parts are enjoying the closeness, and his body parts are coming alive too. I feel his maleness grow against my lower back. He moans and extends his arm down my leg and slips his hand between my thighs. It is so delightful and so scary. I just don't know how to react; who is he with in his dreams? I know I need to wake him, and it will be awkward, but this isn't my doing so far.

I slowly roll over to face him. and he opens his eyes. Gosh, he is sexy. His eyes close and then pop open again. I put my finger on his lips for quiet and point at Caroline on his other side. His eyes came right out of his head when he realizes not only where he is but that he is sexually aroused, and arousal is pressed against me.

First, he smiles, and then, he blushes. I didn't know boys blushed, but he did. He leans in and kisses, me and I feel his arousal again.

Kurt whispers, "I don't want to leave, but I think it's best. If your bodyguard finds me here, well, I don't want to find out the consequences." He leans in, presses all of him against me with desire, and kisses me once more.

There is no question what he wants. I can't help the moan that I whisper into his hair. It is returned with another hungry kiss.

Caroline stirs as he runs his hand across my leg, my stomach, and lingers on a breast. He kisses me again.

Caroline's voice breaks the silence. "Bloody Hell!, You two should get a room and not mine."

Kurt's eyes sparkle as he purrs. "Best threesome a guy could have." Caroline throws her pillow, and Kurt catches it as he bounds to the door. He stops at the door and winks at me.

I am sure I blushed. When will I learn to control that? The door opens, and I hear male voices, "Hey Kurt, long night?"

Then Kurt's answers, "Best threesome ever." everyone howls.

Seconds later, Sean comes flying in the front door. He skids to a halt in front of me at my door and says "Come with me." I turn to close the door and get to dressed. I change quickly and meet Sean on the porch. Outside, we walk around the side of the big porch and sit on the swing.

"Did you go in through the window last night?" Sean growls.

I step back and say,"One of your guys was shadowing me, so you know I did."

"That's the thing," Sean spits out, "my guy was stopped and could not catch up with you. He was unable to follow you because your Kurt friend decked him."

I blanch because I had felt safe climbing in. I look up, "So you didn't see Kurt come in the window either."

Sean puts both his hands on my shoulders and says "I want to know everything, every detail".

Fat chance, he can have the basics but not every detail.

This summer can't end fast enough because, I can't wait to dance on the show. I want to dance. I will have to keep Caroline's words in my head, "If you want it, go get it." I will miss the everyday friendship of Caroline and the long talks about everything. Caroline is going to a private boarding school outside Philadelphia. I will be in a Catholic High School in Hagerstown, Maryland. We have pledged to write every day. I hope she keeps up her end, I know I will keep up mine.

Caroline does write all summer, and I do too. As Labor Day approaches, she tells me she is going to Ocean City, Maryland again with her sister, she asks if I can come. I want to, but I can't get anyone to listen, long enough to make it happen. If my parents were home, I know they would listen, but Sean and the others are busy getting Lucy back to boarding school, and me to my new high school and scheduling my time at the television studio in Baltimore that a side trip to Ocean City just isn't going to happen.

I write to Caroline to say I can't come. I send one letter to her home in DC and another to the beautiful Victorian house in Ocean City. I don't know exactly when she will be there, so I wait for a reply. Nothing comes. Labor Day is one day away, no letter. I hope she isn't angry. Labor Day comes and goes, and I hear nothing. So unlike Caroline.

FOURTEEN

LANGLEY OPS

- Assignments for Big Bird and Whitey's girls are as follows while they are out of the country.
- Tiger detail will be the same as last school year.
- Kitten's friend Caroline was in a car accident and intel is being gathered on her condition.
- Kitten's detail is much more complicated on the weekends but during the school week should be fairly routine.
- Read carefully and see me if changes need to happen.

FIFTEEN

No Boarding School for Me, St. Maria Goretti

DANCING ALLOWS ME TO BE alone with the music in the middle of hundreds of people. The studio we tape in is so cool. I love the clothes, especially the white shiny go-go boots. Yep, my favorites are the white shiny ones with big chunky heels. I want to be the stereotypical teen, long hair to mid-back, and thin as a rail. Twiggy is all the rage, even though I am just that way naturally. I see other girls work hard to be like the supermodel. I am 5'8", tall for a girl, especially since my mom was just 5'2" in heels and her four sisters are shorter than she is. I do work hard to get my long hair rolled in orange juice cans to make it straighter, then iron it between two damp towels.

Mini-skirts and really wide-legged bell bottoms are the norm for the show. I like the mini-skirts and boots. I have nice muscular legs, so I rock that look. During the school week. I wear a uniform. It is a navy-blue wool blazer and skirt that goes to my knees with a white button-up shirt and saddle oxfords. In the warm months we lose the blazer and add a pinafore, which is made of fabric that is called pillow ticking. It is blue and white striped. I know it's very old fashioned, but I think it was the height of fashion for Catholic schools especially pricey ones. So, all the cool clothes given to us on the show to wear are just like being in heaven. Sometimes the other kids complain about what they are wearing, but I am sooooo glad for Friday afternoons because no uniform for me. I change on the way.

My routine for the show is for a driver to take me to the taping.

It is usually one of Sean's friends Dean, Mike or Joe that stay with me, then drive me back home. I guess they are really agents like him but younger and I am their easy assignment.

I have made a deal with Mom and Dad that if I didn't have to go back to any boarding school, then I agreed to only do school activities and dance. They agreed. Well, another condition on their part was I had to listen to the nanny—yes nanny/cook/housekeeper. So, I decide to pretend she is my personal assistant. Since she looks like a personal assistant, it is easy. Plus, she treats me with respect and won't let me hide as a child but stand up like a young adult. I really like that, and I need that. She is thirty something with dark brown hair that is much shorter than mine. She is not thin but not fat, just okay. I hardly noticed at first all the muscle and true physical fitness that is under her clothes, but it is there.

I also have agreed not to leave Sean or his friends when I am out. It crossed my mind not for the first time that it is weird that I always have one of dad's friends with me, even when Dad and Mom aren't there. It is the 60's, and we do have air raid drills, protests, and riots happening daily. Vietnam is ever present, so having someone armed, who is nice and big and strong, felt safe. My dad thinks of everything.

I still haven't heard from Caroline, so I write her again.

With the deal made, I start my freshman year at St. Maria Goretti High School. I soon fall in a routine where school and dancing consumes my days. The rest of the world is a totally different thing. My mom and dad talk at lot when they are home, and I so my best to listen. My parents seem like real friends, and I am fascinated with that. I want a real friend like that. Wait, I have that in Caroline. Why hasn't she written?

I have met many of my peer's parents, and most are less than nice together. I mean alone, they are nice adults, but together it is tense.

My parents travel a lot, hence I spend lots of time with the nanny or my personal assistant as I like to call her, Diane is her real name. I am not allowed to just sit down and listen to my parent's conversations, so I hide on the stairs just out of view. At thirteen, I am not included in their quiet moments, even though I think they should include me.

My parents sit close together, speaking low and sweet to each other. Then, other times, they really are saying how they feel about their ideas, not arguing but trying to persuade each other. They tend to forget I am around and just have long discussions. My parent's conversations range from the rough skin on the bottoms of Mom's feet or the color of the curtains, to US putting troops in Vietnam, or the march on Selma, and France withdrawing from NATO (I had to look that one up I didn't know what NATO was). The six-day riot in Los Angeles, or Israeli and Arab battle over the Gaza strip (Why anyone wanted that strip of land I couldn't say), or China detonating a hydrogen bomb or did the lawn need watering.

Going to a Catholic school does two things. You pray a lot. It also shelters you from many things. For me, I visit the real world twice a week and dance.

SIXTEEN

LANGLEY OPS

- Whitey and Big Bird initiated a check on Caroline and family results in your packet, Sean has been notified.
- They will leave for South America soon, this situation my delay that departure.
- Sean will give us a go date.

SEVENTEEN

Caroline

———

THE REAL WORLD COMES BOUNDING in the door with a long-distance phone call from Washington DC. Sean calls Dad to the phone. I can hear his voice change in tone. Something is wrong. Dad calls Mom to the kitchen. Me, I am in the den trying to read. The hushed conversation has a weird vibe to it. The conversation is in hushed voices. I can't make it out. I decide to put down the unread book and casually walk into the kitchen to get a drink and find out what is so important. I push through the swinging door to the kitchen. Everyone stops talking, turns and looks at me. Okay this is weird.

Mom comes over to me and hugs me and says she is so sorry. "Sorry about what?" I ask.

Dad comes close and very slowly and gently tells me, "Caroline hasn't written you because she was in a very bad car accident. Her sister is still in the hospital and will be there for a while. Caroline did not survive."

"What?When? How? No." I can't breathe. I slump down and just sit on the floor.

Dad kneels over and then sits down next to me. "Emmy things like this will happen all your life. With that said it is not easy to lose someone important in your life."

Mom follows and sits on the other side. I put my head on her shoulder and cry. How is it fair to find a friend and then they are taken away? Did God think I didn't need her, deserve her. It has been so hard to talk to people my age and she taught me that.

I listen try to the details, but I am in shock. The short of it is, she was with her sister, and they were all drinking and driving and the car accident took five of the six kids. I know Caroline's sister will never be the same, and neither will I.

There is no funeral to go to, because it has already happened. Mom and Dad listen to me tell them about my friendship and how much I will miss her. I tell them that Caroline's words gave me courage to dance. Mom says her words will give you the courage to go to High School even though she will never get to do that. I look at both Mom and Dad and tell them I will use her words to get what I want and make her proud. They smile. I know I will cry when I get to my room, but for now I tell Mom and Dad I am going to get ready for school tomorrow. I stay in my room and am just numb. Caroline gone. How can one year and one girl have so much impact on my life, but it has. I miss her, she was my rock and my roll.

I like school and have always done well. St Maria Goretti in Hagerstown is a great little school. At St Maria Goretti I enjoy being with about fifty kids in each grade level. At Frederick Academy of the Visitation, there were eight girls in my eighth grade class, Caroline was one of them. I had gone to school with most of these kids before at St. Mary's when I spent a few years in Elementary school. So being back with my friends is such an unexpected feeling of security, especially after the bombing and losing Caroline. I need this. A lot.

I join the Drama Club and try out for cheerleading. I am successful in both. I also try out for the lead in the school musical, "Bye Bye Birdie". I think I will be perfect for the lead, Kim McAfee, but the director thinks a friend, Cathy, will be better. Of course she is wrong, But, oh well, I am cast as the "best friend", go figure.

Gary Arcideacano, aka, "Archie" is my first real boyfriend. I met him years before, as a kid in grade school, but as a freshman, he has changed into a totally hunky guy or is it me or is it me? I turn around to exchange math tests, so we can check them, and there he is. Just staring at me. I think I am staring too. Oh God does he see me staring? Of course, he does. Keep control, and for Pete's sake, don't blush. We exchange papers. He smiles. I smile and that is that. After school that day, as I am leaving play rehearsal, I look up, and there he is. This time, I do blush. He asks to walk me home. I tell him I don't walk home. But I can walk home with him and my ride can pick me up there. He looks surprised and confused and says "sure".

I am not sure when we fell into a routine, but I would finish after school drama rehearsal, then walk to the baseball field on campus where he was coaching young kids in baseball. I wait until he finishes. Then, we would walk to his house. I love this time with him. I feel that, I have found the friend I want like the friendship I see in my parent's relationship, how they enjoy being with each other.

He lives four looong blocks from the school, in a big house with a grand porch that wraps around the whole first floor. Those four blocks brought many firsts for me. First time to hold hands with a boy, first boy who asked me to be his official girlfriend, not my first kiss - but my first kiss that lasted so long I lost track time. I just know I could hardly breathe when he released me. I love sitting on the porch swing listening to him talk while waiting for my ride home.

His mom is simply amazing. When we arrive, she brings out cookies and lemonade, I feel like I am in a movie or maybe a sitcom. I can always smell dinner cooking. His five younger brothers are everywhere, playing boy games, chasing each other, building forts in the tree or bushes, playing cops-and-robbers, and on and on. I think he is a little embarrassed at times, but not having brothers, I am soaking it all in. I just love starring in my personal love movie. every girl wants to be Cinderella or Sleeping Beauty but I want neither I have a new one writing itself as each day goes by. Maybe someday I will write it down, for now I am going to enjoy it. Caroline told me to live in the moment, so you can relive it later when in need. I am.

The swing is where we practice kissing. It is also where we hear that age-old song from his brothers "Emmy and Archie kissing on the swing, K-I-S-S-I-N-G." First comes love, then comes marriage, then comes the baby in a baby carriage". They laugh and sprint away. If they got too close, Archie will give them "nuggies", —you know when you rub your knuckles back and forth across someone else's head. That only happened once. After that, they were too smart to come too close.

My personal "love movie" lasted almost a year but came to a tragic end one fall afternoon during sophomore year. I lost control of my love movie, I wanted our story to go differently but sadly it didn't. The last day I ever saw him was such an amazing day. I decided the night before I want to grow old with him.

Archie sits with me at lunch, kisses me in front of all of our friends, and hands me a friendship ring. He says, "I will always own a piece of your heart but you will own all of mine."

This declaration is in front of our friends. It is more than I ever expected. I put the ring on and cry. I don't even have words, I just kiss him. I am so embarrassed but also so happy. We are in all the same classes, so at the end of the day, we go to our after-school commitments, anticipating our walk home, our quiet time eating cookies, and holding hands on his porch swing.

It is a sparkling October day. The big trees by the school are thousands of shades of orange and yellow. Some of the leaves float in the breeze. As I arrive at the ball field, I can see he is practicing batting with the youngest little boys. I think the group are six and seven-year-olds. The boys at this age swing a lot and hit the ball only once in a while. There is a lot of chasing the ball and then getting it back to Archie to pitch again. He smiles at me and then turns back to pitch. He does and the little boy at bat hits the ball square-on with a loud, solid crack. This little man is so surprised he hit the ball. Seconds later, it hit Archie in the forehead. He drops like a rock. Everyone runs toward him.

I thought he was dead, but he sat up and smiled. Then he said, "I think it is time to walk home."

Some of the parents wanted to drive him home, but he refused. He tells them this lovely girl will escort him home. I smile he means me.

We got his stuff together and began our four-block walk. As we walk, he stops to kiss me three times. Not the small, little pecks he would sneak at school, but long, breathtaking, intense kisses, body-to-body kisses. I have never been kissed so thoroughly before and I could kiss him all night long like that. I have never had such a strong urge to take off all my clothes and continue with anything else he wanted to do ever.

I tell him, "I love you."

He kisses me, and smiles, and says, "I know, and I love you to the moon and back. Our moon that shines on us at night."

As we arrive at his porch, his mom is standing there, waiting on us. One of the moms had called her. She has an ice bag for him, and my ride is waiting too. I found out later she had called and asked the driver to come get me early. My mother met me at the door to my room the next morning. I didn't even know she was home. That is when my nightmare began.

"You will not be going to school today. Archie was taken to the hospital last night."

I told her we needed to go see him. She smiled, not a happy smile, but a sad one. She sat me down on my bed and very quietly told me, "Archie died last night of his head injuries."

I didn't know what to do. I knew that couldn't be true because he is mine. So, he *couldn't* be gone.

I turned around and went back to bed. I don't remember eating or sleeping. All I remember is crying. My parents allowed me to grieve.

SEVENTEEN

Langley OPS

- Kitten team needs to be conscience of her moods and give privacy as much as possible, but stay close in case she needs you.
- Other teams are same.

EIGHTEEN

Archie My Love

———

I AM HERE AT ARCHIE'S, FUNERAL but not really. St. Anne's Catholic Church is kind of new. The seats are filled with people like Sunday mass. Who are all these people?

I walk all the way to the front over to his family. His family is so quiet. His brothers all hug me, so does his mom. His oldest younger brother, he is ten, whispers in my ear, "Archie said he is you knight in shining armor, I could be that if you want."

I can hardly gulp out an answer, "I'd like that. Thank you," and I kiss him on the cheek.

He backs away with a knightly bow. Archie's mom reaches me then and holds me so tight for what seems like an hour. She finally pulls back and sits me down on the pew beside us. People around us seem to disappear. She stares into my eyes. I see Archie there. I freeze.

She whispers, "Archie loved you. I know you loved him too. I am so glad he had you and experienced true love. You will always be in my prayers.

Tears rained down my face. I hugged her back. After that moment, I only have sketchy memories of the rest of the day.

My room seemed like the only safe place. I dreamed about my fairytale with Archie. After a week or so, I know, I went to school but I don't remember what went on. They replaced me in the play, and I didn't even notice.

I came back to reality the day before Thanksgiving when I heard my mom on the phone telling someone she was going to take me to a psychologist because I wasn't talking at all. She hung up the phone. I need to end her worrying about my mental health. She needs to know I will be okay.

"Mom, I am just sad. I had a fairy tale relationship with Archie and it didn't have a happy ending. It isn't necessary for you to worry about my mental health. I will be okay in time and right now I am quiet because I just don't have anything to say."

I hug her and start to head back to my room when she grabs me by the shoulders, looks me in the face, smiles and says, «There are lots of fairy tales and you can have more than one. Be patient but never forget this one. This one was a great one hold it tight but go on and live. He would want that."

I cried. My mom held me until my tears stopped. We went out to the sun porch and snuggled under a blanket. I fell into a much needed deep sleep.

Being in a class of fifty kids means you know everyone, and everyone knows you. There is no need to tell people how I feel or listen to them. It just is what it is. We all grieved together. During that sad time, I took tests to graduate early. I wanted an escape so it was easy to lose myself in studying.

I pass all the required tests, and I am scheduled to graduate May of 1968 instead of with the class of "70. This would be easier, all of Archie's friends and mine would be there and he wouldn't. My classmates would not even know that I have graduated early.

I am just fifteen, so no one even guesses I can graduate early, but I did. I want out of here. I have to go to school so stay with my original classes. November to May I can do it.

NINETEEN

LANGLEY OPS

- Miller family has been vetted, no big problems there.
- All the other teens have been vetted with and emphasis on Edward Lysinger.
- No red flags at this time.
- Big Bird and Whitey are in Spain and then back to Paraguay.
- Tiger is still at FAV all is well there.

TWENTY

Eddie

ONE OF MY GIRLFRIENDS, TOOTSIE Miller, yes, that's her real name, has a brother, Bob. everyone calls him that except his mom who calls him Robert. He is a senior in the Class of '68. He is a handsome, tall blonde with a body to die for, making him the most popular boy in school Truth be told, I lust after him, and so did every other girl.

Tootsie invites me to her house for a sleep- over. There will be four of us. I hope to see the real Bob, not the totally put together guy from school. When I am at Tootsie's house, I begin to realize she and her brother are actually good friends, not just siblings. Again, I find myself wishing for a good friend like that. Wow, I think that relationship is cool. My sister and I are not friends not like that, not at all. I don't have any brothers or even good friends that are boys. Note to self. Maybe boys can be friends. Bob Miller seems like the perfect brother and friend. He always has guy friends over, and all of them are just beautiful.

I just sit and daydream about what it would be like to be in Archie's arms again. Tootsie is getting things ready to play cards, but I have slipped into my mind again. This time, I am not grieving so much as I am examining the four boys there to play cards with us. Is it to soon to notice them? Am I forgetting Archie? Is this feeling okay? when will I figure this out.?

First, there is Michael aka Mickey, he is 5'10" or so and muscular, I think he lifts weights. He is the quiet one. Then Matt, he is the seductive one, he loves coming in real close and whispering in your ear. Rounding out the quartet is Eddie, he is 6' and has a young Elvis look going on. He rocks that. These three are Bob's friends and all such fun to look at. How nice would it be to look into their eyes and see desire look back. I had that with Archie and want it back.

Take Eddie for instance, he is tall dark and handsome. Just then Bob turns on the music and there is an Elvis song playing *Can't Help Falling In Love with You*. What a sensual song. That is a perfect song and I visualize Eddie looking deep into my eyes singing that to me. I see him move in close and hold me close. I close my eyes waiting for his lips to meet mine. I am deep in my dream when Bob asks who I want as a partner. I look up startled. Can he read my mind?

Bob repeats the question, "Who do you want as a partner?" He smiles his sexy little smirk. "You have four men to choose from. It can't be that hard."

Matt chirps in, "Maybe we need to give you our credentials or assurances we are qualified in many areas of expertise." As he waggles his eyebrows up and down.

I thought Matt, a six-foot something cutie has a girlfriend but who knows. I smile and blush trying to stop my naughty daydream and try to answer. Bob is talking about cards not what is in my head. I search for and answer trying to look natural and not like a deer in the headlights. Eddie is the first to softly smile.

I nod and say. "I take Eddie".

He smiles and I feel warm all over. It is nice. Matt comes close sits down throws his arm around me and declares I have made a mistake.

"Guys, everyone knows I am the pick of the litter," Matt declares.

Bob says, "Nope, the little lady has picked Eddie from the litter. Let's see how Eddie handles this challenge." Everyone laughs.

Am I the challenge, or is Eddie? It's only cards. Right? Right.

Eddie is a really nice guy and a senior. He is tall, lean and handsome like a young Elvis. No wonder I turn to Eddie and hear Elis in my mind. This new realization that boys can be friends, and not necessarily boyfriends, made coming to Tootsie's house so intriguing. Thank God for Tootsie's influence, I might someday be normal again.

Later, Bob says, "Let's take a break, get drinks and swim."

Tootsie and I go to the Pool cottage and change for our late night swim. I don't think I have ever been in a pool at night especially with boys. The pool is so beautiful with just the soft landscaping lights on and the lights in the pool but not the big ones that lite up the place like a basketball court. It is just pretty. Tootsie and I sit down by the pool with our feet dangling in the pool. Tootsie asks, "Are you ready to go out with anyone? I mean is it too soon? You know after the death of Archie."

I swallow hard and look down at my hands. "I guess so. It might be awkward for me at first, but I know I need to move forward even if it is not my choice."

This led to her next question, well not so much a question but request. "Will you go on a date with me and my boyfriend, my brother and his girlfriend, and our friend, Eddie."

Crap, she just said Eddie. Was she in my head too. Is it written all over my face? I slip back to Eddie in my daydream, those eyes those sweet curve of his lips.

Tootsie leans over and whispers "Emmy where are youcome back to earth."

Okay I blush again and speak quickly, "Tootsie, for you, yes. Besides my parents will back off, if I do what they think is normal. Does Eddie know?"

Tootsie smiles and blushes. Her next words surprised me. "Eddie has seen you with me at school and has asked about you. He thinks you are cute and fun. I told him you are still healing from the loss of your best friend. He doesn't know much more than that. At least not from me. Don't get me wrong. He did ask I just told him it is your story to tell, not mine."

My daydream is turning into reality.

Eddie appears with the other guys, but he sits next to me and says, "You're good at cards, right?"

I nod. He smiles.

We swim and talk and play cards. It is so nice. That song keeps coming back in my mind *Can't Help Falling in Love with You*. I just feel silly because I hardly know him but the emotional pull to him is overwhelming. When I talk to Eddie, I think there is hope I will find that forever friend. He is a gentle soul and so sweet. He did not know Archie, hearing about him through Tootsie's brief description.

This developing relationship takes me away socially from the rest of the sophomores, and most of the grief we are enduring together. Being with Eddie is like opening a new door to another life and leaving the hurt and pain behind. Is that cheating, hiding or surviving? I don't know. I can just feel myself healing. Eddie is making that happen even if he does not really know what's happening inside my head. I am conflicted. Should I tell Eddie how he is affecting me. Eddie also doesn't know I am graduating with his class. Wonder if he'll think it is a problem? Maybe he would be surprised and proud but I am not sure. Should I tell him? In my head, I can hear my mom saying "Don't let a man know how smart you really are. It only causes problems." I just don't know how to feel.

Even after I pass all the required tests, my choice is to still go to class as a sophomore. It is so much easier to just exist and not have to think so much. There are moments that the memories of Caroline and Archie are still so fresh, so painful.

There are days that are so long, the sorrow of losing Archie overtakes me. Then there are days when I realize the world is moving on and so must I. Archie has been gone since the first week of October. It feels like yesterday and then it feels like I am forgetting what he looked like. I try to remember his sent; I can't it makes me cry. There are times I smell food cooking and I remember the lovely fragrance from his mom's kitchen as Archie and I sat on his porch.

It's now almost Christmas. I have days that the real pain of the past and the loss of Archie stop me dead in my tracks. I feel Archie's presence when I see his photo and the ring that hangs around my neck. I love touching the ring especially when I have a moment of crisis. There are small moments at school when I feel the greatest need for that touch.

Karen Wilson gets great pleasure in telling me that she is tired of seeing the ring. She says I am milking it for sympathy she wonders why I can't move on. I think I will never stop needing that memory of love that I get from that small touch. Eddie has never asked me whose ring it is. I know he sees me touch it. If he asks me, I will tell him no matter what Life goes on and so must I.

Eddie and I are going to the Christmas Dance at school. I am a little worried about what my classmates will say. It has been eleven weeks since Archie was buried, almost three months. This is our first time out in public with my younger classmates. Some have seen me in the mall or at church with Eddie, but I have always been in a group.

The dance is at the Knights of Columbus Hall, next to the church and school. We arrive together all ten of us, Eddie and I Tootsie and her boyfriend Ted, Bob and his girlfriend Mary Claire, Mat and his date, Carol Ann and Chuck with Susan. Someone has spent hours making it beautiful. Normally it looks a giant "Plain Jane" space. The walls are covered with white sparkling paper that move ever so slightly. This light breeze and the soft lights on them give it a feel of a winter night. There is a star up high, it is supposed to be the North Star that led the Three Kings to Jesus. The life-size nativity figures over by the doors that lead to the church walkway are just lovely and peaceful. The tables and chairs are covered with a sparkly silver fabric. Each table has candles and pine wreaths as the center pieces. None of the overhead lights are on so the candlelight and lights behind the draped paper covering the walls give you the feeling of being outside on a winter night.

Tootsie does a 360 as she marvels at the decorations. Her eyes keep looking at everything which makes me look too. We Jon hands and slowly spin enjoying the winter wonderland. We stop, giggling and realizing that this wintery world is so much better than the school gym could ever be.

Our group is almost all seniors. Tootsie her boyfriend, Ted, Bob and his girlfriend, Matt and his date, Chuck and his date, and Eddie and I. Our group of star-studded entourage approach the side of the room where Bob's crowd has staked out a few tables in the back corner. I notice, we are a large group of twenty, how fun.

Before we can arrive there Eddie takes my hand, leading me to the dance floor for a slow dance that has just started. He can dance. My heart sings. I love to dance. This is just one more reason to love Eddie. The song ends, and we head for the table. Father Michael approaches us. I know Father Michael but it is evident that Eddie knows him well by the hug instead of a handshake. They speak quietly, Father smiles at me, he is wishing us a Merry Christmas. Then we continue to the table. The others are chatting and leaning into each other. I am enjoying their company, but my eyes linger on the dance floor.

I look back and Eddie is smiling, "Dance?"

I want to slow dance again with Eddie. He really can dance. I ask him "Who taught you to dance, because you can dance."

He smiles and says, "My Mom, she is the best."

It's obvious his Mom is a good dancer. Everyone is heading to the dance floor and so are we, my heart sings again. As we clear the other tables, on our way to the dance floor, Karen a sophomore in my class and her small group of girlfriends are the first to approach us. Karen is the fashion police of our class, and she can be sweet or just awful. I smile and make eye contact, she smiles back, but it is on her lips, not in her eyes.

I look around for Tootsie, this feels wrong. This could be an ambush—she is famous for that. I think my outfit will pass her inspection. I look down, I am in a plain little black dress with a red corsage. At that moment, Tootsie and her date appear out of thin air, thank God. I look at Eddie he obviously doesn't know this group. This could be good or really bad. I don't know what to do. I squeeze Eddie's hand; he looks down at me and then back to Karen. I feel the air stir around me. It is a pine sent in the air mixed with the wax burning from the candles on the tables. Everything slows down, I feel Tootsie move in close and so does Eddie I try to formulate a sentence that will be friendly and not give away how freaked out I am.

Karen uses her loud gooey-sweet artificial voice, "You sure didn't wait long to seduce another one, Archie is hardly cold."

The sound and people seem to stop to listen.

I don't move, I am stunned. Her cruel words are like a knife in my heart. I am worried about my dress, but she is here for the kill.

My first instinct is to reach out and slap her, no I want to strangle her, maybe kill her. That would stop her. I want to cry it hurts so bad. Why is she so callous, ruthless, heartless? I guess all those lectures Father Michael and the nuns have put us through meant nothing to her. I'll be damned if she will see me cry.

Wait, is it too soon? Should I not be here? Is this too soon to be out on a date? I haven't really been alone with Eddie. We've always been in a group. We are still in a group. She will not see me cry. Tootsie's date takes my hand and starts to lead me away.

Eddie leans into me. "Go with Ted, I will be there in a minute"

As I walk away, I can see Father Michael in the distance. He looks angry; dare I say, "Hot under the Collar". Oh yeah, he is on a mission. I am sure he will stop this.

Tootsie. in her stage voice, announces "Karen Vaughn, you have some nerve accusing anyone of having too many men in their life. It will take me hours to list all the many boys you have *BEEN* with. Do you want me to start now? Because I will." All the girls with Karen seem to fade away when Tootsie spoke.

I look over my shoulder. No one moves. Ted says, "Come on Emmy, it will be okay." I want to listen

Then I hear Eddie's sultry voice. "Tootsie, this girl is a sad, jealous, little girl. Walk away." Eddie spoke with a low, guarded, quiet voice, so calm, it was scary.

He turns and says loud enough for anyone, well everyone really, to hear. "Merry Christmas Karen, to you and your friends. I am sure your incorrect observation of Emmy's social life is not meant to be so cruel, but it is. An apology to Emmy is not necessary, she truly understands your sadness over Archie's death and knows you are grieving too. I will pray for you. If you turn around Karen, I think Father Michael, is coming and I think he wants to visit with you and your friends. If you will excuse me now, I am going to dance."

I must look awful to Eddie. I feel awful, I need a hug, one that will last forever.

Eddie walks over to me and leads me to the dance floor. He holds me in his arms, and we dance. I melt into him. The music finally enters my head. It is Bing Crosby singing *White Christmas.*

I also notice, Tootsie and Ted, Bob and his date Mary, plus Bob's group their dates have joined us on the dance floor. They have surrounded us, and I feel like the wagons have circled up for protection. I am so glad to have real friends who are friends in the good times and bad. I nestle myself into this strong man's arms and dance. Tonight, Eddie is my hero.

The spring semester was busy socially. Well I was kept busy. This schedule did a lot to keep me looking forward and in constant grief. Eddie and I go to the Sadie Hawkins Dance, Valentines dance, the Prom and all the senior parties, not to mention all the sporting events Bob Miller is in. Eddie plays basketball, but not much else, and he plays the guitar. With Eddie's help, I can smile again, and his gentle kisses are nothing like my memories I feel air movement, a pine sent in the air and wax burning from the candles on the tables of Archie's but I feel so safe.

There are times I have a war going on inside. All these events are things Archie and I would have attended. Am I with Eddie or Archie? Both men make my heart jump, not to mention all my girl parts. Archie is gone, I know it, but Eddie is here, and I care deeply for him. I am so lucky.

When school ends, and I go to Eddie's and Bob's graduation as a guest, even though I technically am graduating too. I have to tell him I am graduating. I don't like lying even if it is by omission. But when is the best time to say something?

TWENTY-ONE

LANGLEY OPS

- Tiger will need a new plan for the upcoming school year. It is in the works.
- Kitten detail at the graduation. Everything went well. We might be over hump on this one.
- Summer plans for Spain are in the works for Kitten, not Tiger.
- Big Bird and Whitey will be in country soon for a much-needed rest.

TWENTY-TWO

Vietnam

———◆———

EDDIE'S NUMBER IS PICKED FOR the draft. Each day of the year is given a number. Number one would be called first and so on. Eddie's birthday is number three. Crap, that means he will go in the first wave at the top of the list. Those first ten numbers will go first. I don't know how this choice thing works.

So, he explains to me, "If I enlist, I get to choose when and where and which branch of service. If I wait til draft report day I have no choice. I will be assigned a branch and a report place. I want a choice. So, I am scheduled for boot camp on the fifth of June."

Why am I losing another man? Maybe he will be shipped off to Vietnam after boot camp. I hope not. It is so scary, a lot of boys are going to Vietnam. I have no words when he explains, I just hold him tight. I realize I am also being shipped off to Spain to college, so we will both be gone for a while. Eddie is going to boot camp— me to school in Spain. It is just another loss. This loss is temporary, not forever. I hope.

My parents have been gone a lot on business the two years I was at St. Maria Goretti. The nannie who cares for me is nice and allows me my space, but she is not Mom and Dad. They are in South America again. The world is focused on Vietnam but my parents are still talking about Nazis and communism in Cuba.

When they are home, I try to listen to them talk. The stairs in our new home make a ninety degree turn halfway up to the second floor. Just as they turn, you can sit unseen and still hear most conversation from the loveseat just below that spot. Mom and Dad like to sit there, cuddle and talk. Sean caught me one night as I sat on the steps listening. They are talking about Franz Stangl and Fidel Castro. As far as I can, tell both are bad men.

Sean stealthily came down the stairs and sits down beside me. I shriek. My cover is blown, and I am sent to my room. Every time they sit there, I think they check that spot.

I feel like an only child, during this time in my life and I think Lucy does too. Lucy is still in the boarding school and loves it there and I am here going to high school in a Catholic high school we only see each other during the holidays. I guess I should be sad about being alone, and I do sometimes, but more often than not, I am okay with it. We have lots of family, so we visit them when our parents are away.

I think Lucy enjoys going to visit my aunt who lives in the Patuxent River area in southern Maryland. Aunt Jean's grand daughter, Linda, goes to boarding school with Lucy, so they travel together. I think Linda and Lucy are close, like sisters should be. Linda has been a pampered child, and Lucy gets that super-attention when they are together. If Linda wants something, she gets it. I mean her nanny, her mother, her father, and her grandmother can't make things happen fast enough.

I remember hearing a story once when Linda wanted a pony and was told no she took hundred dollar bills from her grandmothers' purse and threw them out the window until she got her way. When they discovered what she was doing and stopped the car, she wasn't even expected to get out and look for money. My Mom and Dad would have whooped me first. Then I would have been looking for the bills, and then, been whooped again. I am just amazed by this story. Lucy says it's true. Yikes!

I like visiting my two aunts, Grace and Doll, in the Washington DC area. They have rules, but are kind and they don't care if I just hibernate in my room. Dottie and Charlie are Doll's kids while Suzie and Tal are Grace's kids. Dottie and Charlie have a pool out back and lots of friends. They are also disinterested in me, I guess pretend I am not there. Suzie and Tal are just the opposite. Suzie and Tal are just bullies. Their favorite pastime is to tease me and/

or frighten me. Once, they tied me up in the basement, and just left me there. I think I was there for five to six hours. When I told Mom about it, I never went there alone again. I think Mom and her sister had a big argument. After that I spent more time at our home in Washington DC with Diane the nanny/personnel assistant.

There are so many holidays we aren't even together. I learned it wasn't the holidays that made a time special. It was the time you spent with the people you cared about. For me, being close to Baltimore makes it easy to get to all the tapings for "The Kirby Scott Show" on time. I enjoy being so close to Baltimore so being there alone is okay.

Graduating early, at sixteen, presents new needs and situations I am not ready for. I know my parents are worried about me and college, mostly because of all the civil unrest and racial problems that seem to be happening. I watch the news too, and all the violence on college campuses looks bad. Is it everywhere? It is hard to tell, but the news makes it look really bad. They think I am a little too young and sheltered to go off to college by myself. Maybe I am, but I want-no, need-to go.

My immediate verbal response for them is "I am NOT". But truth be told, I am not so sure. They are *sure* this is going to be *perfect*. I totally freaked out the day they told me. My parents decide to send me to Spain to a University with a priest as my chaperone. Yes. Spain. Notice I am not asked, I am told.

I am not concerned about being so far away from my family. I feel like I have been trained to cope my parents not being around all the time. It is the dancing I am freaked out about. I do not want to give up my spot on the show. It takes the typical teenage snide remarks and stomping to my room and slamming the door to get their attention, but eventually like everything else that is solved. I am to be gone while there is no taping going on. Okay, I can breathe again.

TWENTY THREE

LANGLEY OPS

- Tiger will spend part of the summer at home while Big Bird and Whitey they are there. Then she will go back to Patuxent Naval Station.
- Kitten is in Spain, with a small one-man detail, plus a chaperonne. Everything should be uneventful.
- She is in a very small town, Salamanca, in northwestern Spain.
- She is also with a cousin Dorothy Howell and a couple of friends, a pair of siblings, Scarlet and Red O'Malley.
- These twins are also assets who need us to loosely check on occasionally, but they should not be a problem.

TWENTY FOUR

Spain

———◆———

MY COUSIN, DOTTIE, AND TWO of her friends are being enrolled with me in the Universidad de Salamanca, near Segovia. There is a famous aqueduct in Segovia, not to mention there is a castle in Segovia where they just finished filming the Zepherilli version of "Romeo and Juliet". I think it will be so neat to see this castle in person and then see the movie. I *really* want to see this castle. The movie is not out yet, but the castle is there, and so close. This version of Romeo and Juliet has real teenager actors as Romeo and Juliet. That has never happened before. I can't wait.

Being on my own and in a foreign country might sound exciting, right? well not so much. My chaperone, a priest, is not my idea of fun. Yeah, Father Joe is nice, but is still a priest. Yikes.

Dottie is holier than anyone I know, except the nuns. Her two friends turn out to be twins, Scarlet and Red. Crazy, right? Both have a color for a name. I discover the O'Malley twins are not really Dottie's friends, but they just went to the same Catholic high school with her. They are what I would call "wild children" and they are two years older than I am. So, they just graduated too. After dating Eddie who is two years older than me, I feel like I am closer to them in mindset than Dottie, is only six months younger than I am. Sadly, all they see are two babies. They love to remind us they are legal, and we aren't.

I try to explain, "I have already graduated."

Red looks at me, "Nice try, you just made that up so we will be friends. As if."

I just stare, "I am not that desperate." I want to prove him wrong about his appraisal of me, but arguing with this arrogant boy give me a headache.

The boys, no men, I have been involved with look at me as a valuable person, not a thing to torment or toy with. I need to figure out how to handle or squash, guys like this silly little boy. Red will learn he has misjudged me. Wait, do I even care what he thinks?

The twins are red heads and very up on fashion. Their haircuts and clothes and music make a perfect teen magazine picture. Scarlet's favorite new song, *Sweet Caroline,* is very catchy, and she plays it on her cassette player over and over and over until I am thinking of killing the cassette player.

I find I am in love, not with them, but their personas. I would love to be their friend, but I am too much of a nerd and sheltered to keep up with them or so they think. Silly them. I'm not shy. I find shy people tend to be selfish people who don't want to share themselves with others. I like to watch people to see if they can be trusted and these two fails. Scarlet is a user and a taker. She only does things that benefit herself. I would hate it if I really needed help, because I couldn't depend on her. Once you get past their aura, there is not much I like.

Scarlet is pretty in a bright red head kind of way. Her clothes and makeup perfectly suit her not to mention she has the perfect body. She has every boy, or man for that matter, ready to do anything for her attention. She is very aware of their attention, loves it, and expects it.

Red, her twin brother, is at least six inches taller than she is, six-foot-one and athletic looking. Not leading man handsome, but still manly looking. I discover my first thoughts about him are correct. He is like the "Scarecrow" from "The Wizard of Oz" because there is not much of a brain in his head. However, I think the Scarecrow was a nicer guy.

Our dorm is called Hernan Cortez about three blocks from the University. It is old and charming and has a window in each room that either looks out onto the street or the interior courtyard. The rooms that look out over the street are loud and not so private. I guess if you wanted to know what was happening in town, it would be perfect.

Thankfully, mine looks out on to the courtyard. You can see a lovely space with flowers, a bench, and a trellis to each window with a fragrant honey suckle vine climbing up to my room. My heart sings as I realize this window has a ledge wide enough to sit and read or study. Honestly, I mostly sit and dream. It looks just like the romantic European movies you see where the two lovers are escaping the world to be alone. I sit in my window and hope my lover comes to rescue me. I think of Eddie and pray for him. I am glad Archie is my ever-present angel. I miss them both.

TWENTY FIVE

Carlos and Caesar

———◆———

EVERY MORNING ALL THE AMERICANS at the dorm all walk the three blocks to school, then back to the dorms for lunch, then to the pool in the afternoon and are expected to study in the evenings. I have never really had to study to pass classes so actually studying is a foreign idea. Funny! I am in a foreign country.

There are other American groups from around the country here this summer, each one has 6 to 8 teens in it. All of us add up to about fifty total. I love to just sit back and watch people. You can learn a lot about them but also yourself.

Red is attractive enough to appeal to all kinds of females, even adult women. It is a learning experience just to watch him work the crowd at the pool. He always leaves with at least one female, if not two, and doesn't come back until after dinner. He gets lots of gifts from his lady friends and is kind of smug about all of it. I mean, he seems to think it's *owed* to him. I just wonder what he does exactly to think he deserves gifts. Does he ask them for gifts? I can't imagine asking someone for a gift, or how I would feel if someone I thought as a friend asked me for a gift. The idea just doesn't make sense to me.

I write every day to Eddie about this crazy menagerie, just so he has something to laugh about. Thank goodness, he writes too. I can feel his worry about Vietnam in his letters and what his part there will be. Too close. Very real. So scary.

Dottie studies at the pool, or at least it *looks* like she is. She is back at the dorms for dinner, before heading to evening mass. Scarlet is really a wild thing. If my parents ever get to meet the real Scarlet, they will never worry about me. Not my idea of a plan, so as you can guess she is Father Joe's favorite and probably his little informer.

Scarlet wears the tiniest bikini I have ever seen. My swimsuit is a bikini too, but it covers *all* the girl parts modestly. Hers, however, is a string bikini, meaning if she moves at all while sunbathing well, you could see a lot. Men look and offer her many nice things. She brags about the college men taking her out to dinner and flaunts jewelry from them.

One evening at dinner she is bragging a little too much.

One of the girls from another group confronts her, "Do you also get money for the sex or just dinner and a few babbles?"

Scarlet turns and punches her in the mouth. I was so stunned when she just hit this girl without any verbal fight. I mean I expected her to go off on the girl, but the punch was so crazy. I had envied Scarlet until then. Wow, what a fight those two had hair-pulling, kicking, and biting.

Dottie got up and left immediately—well, as soon as the two were pulled off each other, I guess, to go talk to Father Joe. Like I said, the "informer". I never envied Scarlet ever again. I always waited until Dottie went to evening mass to go out, so she has nothing on me to inform about.

Come to find out, Father Joe who seems very old is thirty-three and is not very attentive to us. I wonder what he does all day. I am used to much more intrusion in my daily life. I feel a freedom the others did not see or understand.

At the pool, there are handsome Spanish boys to watch, but I *dream* of Eddie. During this three-month time, I write Eddie every day. I really miss him. I worry about him. I do not even know where he is.

He writes every day and my parents, bless them, send his letters on to me. I tell him everything, and he "listens" to this sheltered girl grow up. In his letters, he is so sweet to me. He never judges, but he tells me what I need to hear and makes me feel like I belong somewhere. I just love him for that, and I tell him no matter, what we will get together when we return. I want to know what kind of love I feel for him. Is it puppy love, just a blind faithfulness? Is it lust for him, and how he makes me feel when we are physically touching each other? Is it friendship knowing, he understands me his letters are amazing? They make me think it is a little of all those kinds of love. I am not sure I would survive here without them, but I need him in person to work through exactly what I feel for him. I am busy here but lonely.

One day, at the pool, Red introduces me to Carlos. I am stunned. Red doing anything for me worries me. What does he want? What is he getting out of this? The fact he notices me has big RED stop signs in my brain all around. I am suspicious of him. What is he up to? He always has a plan that gets him something, so what gives?

Red says, "Emmy thinks she can run with the big kids. What do you think, Carlos?"

I look from Red to Carlos, trying to figure this out. I have seen Carlos many times here at the pool. He is very popular and knows everyone. I have watched him through my lashes many times. Carlos is about my height, nice looking, and very polite. He smiles a devious smile. Carlos nods at me and says, "Hello Emmy." He points at the chair next to me and asks, "May I sit down"?

I nod. He sits and suddenly I see many eyes looking my way, when he sits. He watches me notice the stares and smiles. "Well, the gossip will begin, I am sorry."

I look up into his beautiful, brown eyes and say, "What are you sorry about? I think you like all the attention and probably the gossip too."

He leans back and laughs. It is a genuine sounding laugh. I relax and smile.

He yells back at Red, who has moved to sit with an older woman. "Red, she's definitely ready to run with the big kids, so no worries."

Carlos might be a nice diversion while I work out what I feel for Eddie.

TWENTY-SIX

LANGLEY OPS

- Carlos Ramos and family are new as Kitten's local acquaintances. They are being vetted now.
- Preliminary reports state his parents own local jewelry store.
- His family have been in Salamanca for decades.
- Big Bird and Whitey in Germany and Paraguay

TWENTY SEVEN

Caesar

———◆———

CARLOS TURNS OUT TO BE the mayor's son, and his Dad owns the most respected jewelry store in town. We talk and swim not only that day but also over the next two days. He is fun to be with if you can get past the evil looks from the other girls.

I like Carlos. He is hot, and I really like being with him, but I am not *dying* for him to kiss me or anything like that. So weird. I like kissing hot guys, but Carlos feels like a big brother or a cousin. So weird. My brain drifts back to Archie leaning into his kisses on the swing on the porch at his house and Eddie holding me while we danced, leaning back to kid me.

He invites me to meet his parents at their home. I am nervous. I wonder if he misunderstands our friendship. He hasn't tried to kiss me but an invitation to his home brings my internal radar in play. His parents are nice but nosey, I answer as many questions as I can but they make me feel cautious.

Dad's words about being cautious ring loudly in my head. "When people try to know too much too soon about you, stop and take a hard look at them. What do they want?"

I am happy when Carlos goes to the door because all the questions stopped. He came back with a drop-dead gorgeous guy. Carlos's dad even gets up and shakes hands. He is introduced as Carlos', best friend, Caesar. His name is pronounced "thay-sar", which is the Spanish pronunciation, not like the name of the Roman ruler. It is the Castilian pronunciation. This man is so hot he smolders. It's like he walked right out of a fashion magazine.

Why is a smoldering, put together man, hanging out in a small town, in the mountains of Spain, instead of in a fashion magazine or something better?

I get the feeling Carlos' mother does not like Caesar, but his dad seems to know him man-to-man. We talk for a short time before Carlos's mom and dad excuse themselves. Caesar seems nice, and he is all in to asking me a zillion questions too. Again, I feel Dad's words wash over me. I will be careful what I share with him.

It is fun to have the full attention of these two hot guys. Floating in the back of my mind is the "Why" are they so attentive. I am not putting out, there are many who would very willingly give in to these hot guys. I push that feeling aside and just enjoy my new friends. Caesar says he is eighteen but he talks much older. Carlos feels like he is eighteen. Again, so weird.

Caesar is an entirely different kind of teenage boy. Yes, he is a tall, tanned, beautiful Spaniard. He says he can dance. But there is something else. I just can't put my finger on it. There is definitely a rivalry going on between these two guys. I think a past competition has just added me to it. I am not comfortable with that idea *at all*.

I like Carlos, but he does not make me tingle when he touches me. I don't have the desire to lean into him and kiss him. I hope he has introduced me to Caesar because he realizes I like him but do not *like* him. I guess it really doesn't matter because I just want - and - need friends to distract me from the overwhelming loneliness I feel.

Eddie is ever-present in my mind. I am constantly reminding myself, even when I am with these two, I need to tell Eddie how much I need him and miss him in my next letter.

I explain to Carlos and Caesar I dance on a show called "The Kirby Scott Show" and it's a popular television show. But I do not tell them dancing is my escape from the loneliness of my world. I don't think they would believe me, but who cares. I miss Eddie, and I also dream of Archie—I miss them both. I wonder if there is room for anyone else. I doubt it. Maybe there is just room for lust.

Caesar is so beautiful and watching him move makes my girl parts come alive. This desire *must* be lust.

Carlos and Caesar invite me to go dancing. Caesar shows up at the dorms to walk me to the club. I don't remember telling them where I lived. Where is Carlos? Is this part of their competition and Caesar won this time?

"Where's Carlos?" I look up into those smoldering, dark eyes. He stops and turns into me.

I hold my breath.

He leans in and breathes into my ear. "*Mi amor, eres toda mia esta noche, pero el estara en el club esta noche.*"

I sigh, take a deep breath to steady my nerves, and tell him what I think he said. "I think you told me Carlos will be there tonight, but I am yours."

He nods and says, "*Todo mia.*" Then, he kisses me.

Wow, can he kiss!

As we end that kiss, I am breathless, and he looks at me like he could devour me. It is more than a little unnerving.

His hand, which is still resting on my arm, slowly slides down to my hand. He lifts my hand to his lips and kisses the top, then my palm, which lights up all my tangled emotions. He turns, and we walk hand-in-hand to a local club called "The Wild Horse". After dancing the night away at the club, Caesar takes me dancing almost every night that I can go.

Carlos is at the club every night too, sometimes with a girl, sometimes not. The girl sits politely and says nothing to me or Carlos. I dance with both guys but mostly Caesar. She, Carmen, dances a couple times with Carlos and never with Caesar. She looks like she is being forced by the look on her face. Is it Carlos that she is unhappy with or does she not like to dance? The guys have three or four drinks but I only drink one Sangria and then water. Caesar tries to get me to drink more but I just son like the taste that much and I know my head will hurt the next day.

"This girl," Carlos whispered in my ear one night, «is to be my bride someday, but she is still too young. She comes with me so we can get to know each other. But as you can see, she hardly speaks"

I am stunned, I look at him "An arranged marriage?"
He nods.
I am speechless. I look at her, and she smiles. I look back at him, dumbfounded.

He whispered again, "She is mine to have unless you will marry me."

I am still speechless because he is serious.

He leans in close and says, "My dad knows who your dad is, and my dad would approve. So, run away with me. I will keep you safe."

My brain goes into over-drive. That last part makes me come back to reality. My reality. My parents, reality. Who is he? Why does he want me? Am I not safe here?

I did not have the opportunity to really answer him or ask what he meant by that because Caesar appears out of thin air. Caesar has a Gardenia in his hands for my hair. He leans over and inserts it behind my ear.

He breathes, *"Mi Amor."*

With those words, Carlos stands and makes Caesar take a step back. Then Carlos steps up close to Caesar. There is a moment of silence before they exchange a fast volley of heated words. They speak in rapid Spanish. Of course, I can't translate it all. I do hear, "she is mine", then," it's her choice", "I am better", "It is needed for it to be me", "I can take her there".

The word "take" makes me nervous. Am I sure he said "take"? I am not sure. This could be more than a simple argument.

They are not quiet and I am sure others can hear. Is this normal?

Finally, Carlos turns quickly, leans over, and seriously kisses me on the mouth. Wow, what a kiss. My brain is struggling to recover from his passion.

He pulls me in close, "Remember, I am here, I am better." Then, he turns to the girl he came with, and leads her away. It is so strange, but also exhilarating to say the least. He sure didn't kiss me like a brother. I am sure his desire is real.

I ask Caesar, "What's that all about?"

"That was Carlos, wishing you were his, but you are mine."

I just look at him. Okay, that's confusing? I am not anyone's.

Well, maybe Eddies', but not either of these guys. I want to go to the dorms. I need to think. I don't belong to anyone. Well, perhaps, Eddie's.

After that night, Caesar brought me Gardenias' for my hair every night. He says the smell reminds him of me. I love the smell of Gardenias, but something in my head is nudging me, like a memory I can't lay my hands on. Oh well, it will come to me. He tells me I am an amazing dancer. I know I can dance—it saves me from my loneliness.

I love my parents. When they are home and we are together as a family, I am so happy. When you finally realize you are all alone in the world no matter how many people are around you, that is when your family becomes important. The bare facts are you are alone in your body. If you let them in and you feel loved, then you feel connected. I feel connected and loved by my parents and even my sister. I also am strongly connected to Eddie, my aunts and uncles and cousins too, but differently. If all of them were here, I think I would not feel so lonely. I see Carlos at the club, and he still speaks to me. I wonder how connected I am with him.He always ends our conversation with a kiss on the cheek and a whisper, *"Podrias ser mio."*

I know this sentence, "You could be mine".

Ahhh, I finally have an answer. I smile return a kiss on his cheek, and whisper, *"No pertenezeo' a nadie,"* meaning: I belong to no one".

When, Caesar and I get up to dance, at "The Wild Horse" club, everyone seems to leave the dance floor, and it's like-we own it. Am I in love or just fin love with the dancing? Gosh, this love thing is so confusing. I miss Archie — he is ever-present in my heart. I feel he is my own personal guardian angel, and he is standing right beside me. I don't share that feeling with anyone, They might think I am plain crazy or have a mental problem.

Eddie is the man who pulled me back to the real world. I think he is my rock. I care —no, worry —no, I need him. Is that so… then, I think I love him.

So, what does that make Caesar? My heart feels warm and excited and safe with Eddie. Caesar makes me sizzle when he touches me, but not *safe*. I probably should worry about this feeling. It feels more like lust, not love with Caesar.One of those warm summer evenings, not so long after Caesar and Carlos's argument about me, things happen. This could be a lovely scene in a movie, except for what happens next.

We are just leaving the club, strolling —well, kind of dancing —down the street when my world changes again.

Walking late at night, with a stunning man, on a small street in Spain, without a care in the world, could be a lovely romantic scene. This is every teenage girl's dream, and it's happening to me. My dream scene pauses when Caesar stops suddenly. Why did he stop? He turns and looks all around us. Is there is someone else with us. I am still worried when he gently leans me against the alley wall.

The movie scene begins again. I can feel my heartbeat faster. He puts his hand under my chin and lifts it, so I am looking into his beautiful eyes. You can drown in those dark sensuous pools. As he steps in close, he just freezes, holding me there for a moment. I can smell his cologne, so familiar. I see the lights dancing in his eyesit is hypnotizing. All my girl parts come alive. I am warm all over. I can *feel* his desire.

He presses against me harder. I can feel his muscles twitch and his breath hitch. He kisses me gently, and I close my eyes. This isn't my first kiss, but it is so good, it could have been.

He pulls back and just smiles at me. "So nice."

I know he is going to kiss me again, and I want him to. Oh I do want him and so much more.

I put my hand on his lips and smile. "I love the kiss, but you need to know I am not going to rush into anything." I hold my breath. I think this might have been my only kiss. He is just standing there a moment not smiling or frowning it feels like forever.To my relief, he smiles and leans hard against me. I can feel all of him, and I do mean all of him.

He is ready for action. His breath is a little raged, then he whispers in my ear, "I will go slow and teach you everything." I tingle all over. I think maybe I do want to go slow and learn everything. Does he mean now?

A trash can bangs nearby, and an alley cat crosses our path. Caesar steps back, just like Sean does when he is on high alert in protection mode. Caesar grabs my hand, and we head for the dorm.

He whispers, "No *segura aqui,* it's not safe here."

I should have known I am being watched by someone other than Father Joe, I haven't seen the priest in a week.

We get close to the dorms, well just around the corner. Caesar leans in again and says, "You go on alone from here."

I open my mouth, to protest.

But, before I can speak, he leans in and breathes, "It's okay, Kitten. We will meet again, be patient."

"What? I know you? Wait!" Caesar is gone; he leaps to a fire escape and ducks in an open window.

TWENTY EIGHT

LANGLEY OPS

- Kitten is being extracted from Spain as we speak.
- Deep Intel on the Ramos family and Caesar Cantera is not good. It is a serious problem.
- Looks like Kitten has been exposed to the Rat Line in Spain, and they are moving to use her.
- Big Bird and Whitey are home from their hospital stay. They are still not up to par, so we are sticking close.
- Tiger will be home soon, joining Big Bird and Whitey

TWENTY NINE

Shipped Home

I GUESS ONCE MY DAD AND mom find out about me discovering this boy, I am shipped home early. It is less than twenty-four hours since my movie scene in the alley with Caesar, and now I am going home. I am supposed to spend more time here, but I am leaving after five weeks. I only got to say Goodbye to Dottie. I wonder what the others will think.

Carlos came to the dorm the next morning, not Caesar. How does Carlos know I am leaving? Last night, I cried when I am told I have to go. The lyrics to that song, by Peter, Paul and Mary, *So kiss me and smile for me tell me that you'll wait for me,* keeps playing over and over in my head. Gosh, how silly can I be?

All of this is still playing in my head when Carlos kisses me and says, "Caesar said he will see you again *mi amor, mi amor hermosa,* so be patient."

Where is Caesar? Why didn't he come to say goodbye? Be calm, and don't spook Carlos because I need to tell Sean who I think Caesar is. Am I right? Who is he really? Now, he scares me. What does he really want?

I smile at Carlos and kiss him on the cheek. I will miss him and I kind of will. Again, my freedom is gone.

My escort home is a older women who is very reserved. Her name is Carol. I tell her about Caesar, and she makes a call before we board the plane. We are on a military jet from Madrid to England, then we board a commercial flight from Heathrow to Dulles, just out of Washington DC. She is not a chatty kind of person, and I soon fall asleep only waking up for meals and restroom breaks. I think I am a chore for her, and I am beneath her to be my escort. This is not in my control or hers.

My long flight home to DC is filled with dreams of Eddie, and Caesar, and Carlos, and even Archie. All I can say is I am so confused. No wonder people don't believe teenagers when they say they're in love. I don't know who I love all, or none, or one, or maybe somewhere in between.

My escort, Carol, perks up when we arrive at Dulles, and she sees the diplomatic limo waiting for us. Inside the limo, is Diane and a man I have never seen before. He asks me to tell him about Spain and, in particular, about the people there. I tell him about Dottie, and Father Joe, and the twins, Red and Scarlett. I then explain about Caesar as well as Carlos, and his family, and the girlfriend. I also tell him Red introduced me to Carlos. I am worried for Red. This man listens as my escort takes notes. Diane prompts me when she thinks I am being vague. The limo takes me to our home in the Georgetown part of Washington DC. The man introduces himself as Mr. Smith. He does not look like a "Mr. Smith". Not sure what a "Mr. Smith" looks like but this is not it. He thanks me, and only I go into the house.

I need to focus on my life and find me. All the way from the airport to home, my brain is filled with swirling thoughts of what my parents will say, Caesar, Eddie, Archie, my friends, my new house, my new neighborhood, my new school. Could my head handle any more? I don't think so.

When I walk in the door at home, I am tired, hungry, and just feeling violated. I want to go to bed and sleep for a week. Jet lag is real, but first, Mom and Dad - just get this over with. I haven't done anything wrong. Then so why was I pulled so fast? I understood why I was pulled to a boarding school when the house was bombed but why now? Caesar and Carlos must be the threat.

Mom hugs me hard but Dad starts the conversation. "What's with this 'Caesar' person. I don't know this man."

"He is a just boy," I shout. I am so tired, but this makes me angry.

Mom follows with, "A twenty-one-year-old is not a boy, but a man."

"He always treated me with respect," I quietly answer.

In my head, I knew Caesar had told me he was just eighteen. Why he lied. How did they know so much about him? Instead I say, "I wanted to stay little longer, at least as long as the others."

This time Dad answers, with a line I have heard before, "You are needed at home."

With that statement, I know there is to be no more discussion. And there isn't.

I have to just sit there and listen to them lecture me about why friends are vetted when I notice Dad looks more than weary. He looks sick —no, injured. Wait, so does Mom.

I look closer, and they notice me looking them over. "What happened to you guys?" Silence, I mean real silence. Finally, Dad says, "We ran into a little trouble on this last trip."

I lean in and look close at them. "You look like a Mac Truck ran over you. What gives?"

It took a minute with some silent communication between the two of them before Mom says, "We were just in the wrong place at the wrong time." She pauses again and swallows hard, I guess seeing that I am not buying that story. Mom looks at Dad again. He nods, and she speaks slowly in a soft voice. "Okay so, we both were caught in a radical gun fight and were wounded but we are just fine."

I am dumb founded. "Injured. Bullets. WHAT THE HELL?"

Mom's shoulders slumped as she began, "We are glad you are home safe, and of course us, too." Her answer makes me freak out.

"Being in the wrong place is like being too close to a sign falling in front of you, not running into gunfire. My danger was an aggressive Spanish teen, but yours was life or death. Do you really put that in the same boat?" I am so loud that Sean appears in the doorway and he is waved away by Dad.

They get up to leave the room

"Wait, I have to ask you guys more questions."

Dad looks back, "Get some sleep, we can talk when you wake up."

I am so angry and worried; I forget to tell them I think I might know who Caesar is. They retreat to their room, and I go to the kitchen. Sean is there, and I tell him about Caesar. While I am talking, he stops chewing his sandwich and stands dead still. He is dialing the phone before I am finished speaking, or even have my peanut butter and jelly sandwich made. He asks me to tell him again, and this time he takes notes.

"This is not a big deal I have already told Mr. Smith." He tilts his head slightly to the left as if I am speaking a foreign language. "You know in the limo with Diane," I add. It is his thinking look.

"Describe Mr. Smith," He says.

I do and he smiles. "Kitten you were talking to our boss. I am glad Diane helped you through that interview. Did you tell your parents?"

I tell him they went to bed before I got the chance. I told him again about Caesar, and he sent me to bed. I heard him dial the phone and ask for Diane as I left the kitchen heading for a soft pillow.

After ten hours of deep sleep and still suffering from a little jet lag, I realize I have much to do.

It is the last day of July,1968. I need to talk to my parents who, by the way, aren't home. Imagine that. I guess they were up early and went somewhere. So, I call Sean.

I need to get my driver's license, learn my way around our new neighborhood, and try to figure out what love is. Fat chance. Okay, license and neighborhood. Two out of three "ain't" bad.

THIRTY

LANGLEY OPS

- Kitten was pulled from Spain. Her team needs to be on their toes.
- She recognized one of the men who befriended her there. She recognized the man, Caesar Canberra, from the hospital after the bombing.
- Intel and photos are in your packages.
- We are trying to figure out why he choose her.

THIRTY ONE

Eddie

―◆―

I HAVE BEEN WRITING TO EDDIE while he is in boot camp. He is getting ready to ship out to who knows where Vietnam? Vietnam really scares me. I hope he is not going to Nam. I love getting his letters, and I really love writing back pages and pages to him. Our plans are to meet up before he leaves.

I am home only two days when I am invited to audition for "Dick Clark's American Bandstand" show, and I jump at the chance. I am really worried I will not be allowed to audition, but, to my delight, my parents make the arrangements. So cool.

My dad does not go with me this time. I go with Sean and Diane. We have to spend the night. It is in Philadelphia, so I need a chaperone. I need to figure out what to wear. I run to my room to write a letter to Eddie I realize I am so shallow. I am writing about Dick Clark and his show and Eddie is talking about Nam. I guess I really am just a silly little girl.

THIRTY TWO

LANGLEY OPS

- Sean and Diane will accompany Kitten to Philadelphia for audition.
- Agents in Philadelphia will clear the way at television Station.
- Tiger is still at Patuxent Naval Station, Lexington Park MD.
- Big Bird and Whitey are still recouping at home.

THIRTY THREE

American Bandstand/Woodstock

I BET YOU DON'T KNOW THAT Dick Clark is a short man. I guess you look taller on TV. I am not sure I like him but his AD, (Assistant Director), Jane, is super. Long story short, I get my audition number. There are ninety-seven dancers here today, I am number sixteen. I close my eyes, take a deep breath, and dance. I hear Caroline in my head, "If you want something, go get it, don't just sit and wait for it." I am doing just that.

I feel good about my number—it is my birth date, and it is the number I would have been in the draft if I had been a guy. Yeah, I know, my life would have been so different if I were a guy. I would be off to Vietnam because of my low number. Bobby Vee and Leonard Nimoy are the guest performers for the show they are taping, and we are auditioning for. It is an eye-opening experience to be up close, watching live performers.

I love Bobby Vee's hit song, *Come Back When You Grow Up Girl*. He is scheduled to sing it today super great. Leonard Nimoy, better known as Dr Spock from "Star Trek" is friendlier than I expected, maybe I am expecting the actor to be the character he portrays on "Star Trek". That old saying, "Don't judge a book by its cover" comes to mind. But what I really learn and lock into my head is they have bodyguards.

I have bodyguards. Hmmmm, so much to think about. This time, I will find out why and make sure I understand why, not just go with the flow. But, right now, I need to dance. Of the ninety-seven dancers, the Baltimore station sent three dancers, and I am one of them. All the others came from all over the country, but mostly from the east coast. I love meeting the other teens from all the other cities. After a lot of dancing and smiling for the cameras, we go get something to eat and wait to find out who has made it. And finally, I have made it to the final group.

The final group will dance on the show being taped today. We are told it is to see who the camera likes. I am in a group with two former dancers, what great luck they have been on the show before and know just what to do. I listen and watch and do as they do. I am in heaven. I zone out and just dance. Even if I don't make it, I will remember this forever. My two new friends are Wayne and Cheryl. They don't realize how nice it is for me to be in their group. Yep, you guessed it I made it.

I decide Dick Clark is not my favorite person at all. If I don't have to talk to him, the better it is for me. I am told three of us will be sent to "Soul Train" sometimes. That suits me fine. It records in the same place and time but on the other sound stage. I thought that you had to be black to be on "Soul Train". I really like the Motown sound. I think "Soul Train" is so much more fun. I am learning a lot about music while on the show - the big buzz is about a concert in New York that is free, outside, and open to whoever can get there. I want to go. Bethel here I come.

There is all kinds of talk about this free concert, close to Bethel, New York. I want to go. I have to think who do I know as well as who can and will go with me? I mean, can they get away and not be noticed, and did I have enough gas and food money without having to ask for it? It is taking a lot of planning and imagination. I ask Tootsie first, but she can't go. The concert is August 15th, and that's when her family goes on vacation. After a lot of thought, four of us are going —Kathy, Karen, Molly and me. We are all military friends, and our families trust each other.

Molly and I live off-base and Kathy and Karen live on base. Kathy lives on base, and her parents have a false sense of control - they think if we are on base, we are stuck and can't leave without them knowing. Kathy's parents are the most laid-back of all our parents, even though her dad is the commanding officer of the whole base. Kathy is also the most independent and well-traveled person I know except for me. We are a formidable traveling team. She is bold and out there, I guess, with her dad always being the boss, it comes naturally. I am the quiet, persuasive one.

My parents are more *diplomatic* in their lives. Kathy always tells me I lie better than she does, and I sprinkle every untruth with sugar that makes it easy to swallow

Karen lives on base too. She is great at research and can read a map better than anyone I know, even me, I am really good. Karen's mom is a nurse, and her Dad is an MP in the navy.

Molly is a family friend of Kathy's, and we all have spent time together at Kathy's house. I don't know her well, but what I do know is good. She is good with logistics, her dad is a high-profile senator, and they are guarded well. She has always had security with her.

While we are planning, Molly examines the poster for the concert. It doesn't say Bethel as the destination, but the concert is called Woodstock. Molly can't find that on the map.

"How are we going to find it? "I ask the group. After much discussion, we finally decide, we will drive to Bethel, New York and just ask.

With Karen's' skill with maps and my Dad's 'triple A membership', I could request a TripTik, we will be okay. I will drive because I have the best car. It is a 1968 Mustang— a sweet ride. While my parents are not home, I ask Sean I can stay at Kathy's' on base. I knew if I am on base, my handlers won't even check on me.

The plan is, I am spending the week at Kathy's. Molly is at Karen house. Karen and Molly will come to Kathy's for a Couple of days. Then Kathy and I will stay at Karen's house. Well only in our notes to parents. Yes, you guessed it. One set of parents think we're at Kathy's, and hers think we are at Karen's. We are really not at Kathy's long, instead, we escape.

We ditch our bodyguards, yeah, I finally realized Sean is a bodyguard. I drive. All of us have "handlers". None of us have ever ditched them, so they are easy to lose — well they just believe us when we say we will be at Kathy's since she lives on a military base. It is just as easy as getting off-base. Kathy's mom is always out doing something with the other officer's wives or taking Kathy's brother to some sporting event. No one pays much attention to four sheltered, giggling seventeen-year-olds. We really look like we are on our way to the park or a picnic. So, when we are asked what we are up to, that is our story. We make a mid-morning run to McDonald's for a milkshake to get off-base and never come back. Freedom.

It is August 15, 1969 and school will not officially start until after Labor Day. We drive north out of Baltimore, towards Harrisburg, Pennsylvania, and then onto Scranton. Some leaves are just hinting at turning colors, but the full fall season will not overtake these beautiful roads until October. The highway from Baltimore, Maryland to Harrisburg, Pennsylvania, has rolling fields and lovely stands of old trees.

Today, the weather is cloudy but not rainy. I have the windows down and love the feeling of the wind lifting my long straight auburn hair. I feel so free, and I am reveling in the moment while I listen to my friend's chatter. There is a lightness to the conversation as only an adventure of this sort could conjure up. We decide to go on the back roads from Harrisburg, which heads us towards Scranton, Pennsylvania. In Scranton where we get out the maps and finish our plan.

If you saw all the maps and heard the arguments that ensued, you would think we are planning an invasion. Molly'sattack plan won out for this invasion, since her plan is best. The radio station's news alert says the New York parkway exit to Bethel is closed. So, if we had gone to the New York parkway, we would never have gotten even close. The police are turning people back at the exit to the farm in Bethel. Of course, with a few wrong turns and missed turns and no street signs, we don't get there until the morning of the sixteenth, but we are excited about our adventure.

As I drive, it rains and rains and rains. In Bethel, we are told the concert is out on some dairy farm. At that point, we are in never-ending traffic. You can only go one way, and there is no place to turn around. I have come this far, so I am determined to get there. I drive some more. I know we are close when there are cars parked *everywhere*. People are *everywhere* too, wet and dirty happy people are *everywhere*. I can't find a good place to park. It is raining harder now. It takes time, but I finally park the Mustang. We all get out. Hearing the music, we walk towards it. As I look over my shoulder at the car, I realize we have a problem —I have parked in a mud hole, and the car seems to have sunk about three inches already. We are going to need help at some time to get it out, but for now, the music lures us on.

As we walk, I am getting very hungry. Our picnic lunch was inhaled along the way. So, all I have is a peanut butter and jelly sandwich wrapped in plastic in my pocket that is smashed beyond recognition. I am wet and muddy and thirsty. I am sure the music is amazing, but I want food and shelter.

The place reeks, and Molly says she is sure it is pot. I don't care, I am just hungry and thirsty and wet and muddy and just starving, so, I eat my peanut butter and jelly smash. It is so good.

I learn firsthand what "free love" is in a very quick and up-close way. I mean I know what having sex is but knowing and seeing are two very different things, especially when you are watching it in the rain and in *public*. My abstract idea of having sex up until now would be very romantic and *in a bed*, but surprise, it's not always like that. I realized they didn't care, they didn't even notice us, and there is a happy ending or at least for him, I think. We walk on and on and on. Soon we see many more people moved by the music, or pot, or just plain lust to enjoy each other publicly. Sometimes, it is not just one-on-one but a group.

Food is nowhere to be found. I wonder why food is my number one priority and I am not concerned about all the sex happening around me. I mean I am just as curious as any other teen, but a juicy hamburger is more important to me right now. Wonder why?

THIRTY FOUR

LANGLEY OPS

- Kitten is AWOL; she ditched her bodyguard and so did the Senator's daughter plus two other girls from the base. So we assume Kathy, Karen and Molly are with her.
- Molly's backpack has a tracker in it, and it is in upstate New York at the Woodstock concert. So, hopefully, the girls are together.
- Sean has a detail on the ground, so we should have them in minutes. But It is time to tighten up security on all these girls.
- Kitten will be returned to Georgetown for her parents to deal with.
- Molly's parents are also in DC, but the other two have parents waiting back at the Andrews Air force base.

THIRTY FIVE

The Going Away Party

MOLLY'S DAD IS A SENATOR, and I found out he had a military tracking device built into her backpack. So, as you might have guessed, we are found. Between that and the TripTik I ordered from Triple A, we are doomed. It is not pleasant. I am so hungry, I digress, I also found out that pot makes you hungry amazing, needless to say, we are all grounded and only are allowed to see each other on base and supervised like little kids. I am lucky I still get to dance but only, because I have signed a contract, and my parents won't break it. Of course, I am never, ever, left alone.

So, when Tootsie calls and invites me to stay at her house for the big send-off party, I want to die. I am so sure they won't let me go. I tell Tootsie my story, and she laughs. I want to kill her. Why is she laughing? Doesn't she understand I will miss seeing Eddie before he goes to Vietnam.

I start to cry, she stops laughing and says, "Look I think I can fix this. Is your Mom at home?" I answer, "Yes, both of my parents are home."

Tootsie says, "Tell your mom my mom needs to talk to her. I will explain to my mom, and I bet she will get your mom to let you come. Don't say what it is about, act dumb. Give me a moment to get Mom on board. You *have* to be here."

I say, "Okay, but I doubt it will work." In my heart I hope, no, pray that it does work.

Tootsie softens her voice and says, "Sorry I laughed, I was

laughing about how silly you girls were at that concert. I am glad I didn't go and get caught, but I am jealous you did get to be there."

Tootsie lays the phone down, and I hear her explaining my problem to her mom. I can hear her mom say she would ground me too for that mess. But I also hear her say this is too important for Eddie, and he would then be the only one without his girlfriend there. Tootsie reminds her mom that is was Eddie who brought me back from my grief over Archie's death. I know her mom knows how careful he is with her healing from her loss of Archie.

Tootsie came back to the phone and said, "Go get your mom. Let's see if my mom can work miracles."

"Okay," I say a silent prayer and call mom to the phone.

Mom sits silently as Mrs. Miller talks. I can feel her tension. I can also feel her expression soften as the conversation continues. Mom looks at me, and a tear is falling down her check. I cry too. I figure she is sad for Eddie, but she has not answered Mrs. Miller, so I figure all I will have are Eddie's letters for comfort since I will not get to see him before he goes. I turn to leave. I will be better in my room alone with my grief.

Thirty minutes later, Mom and Dad come to my room. I am ready for the "Sorry, you can't go because life has consequences' talk. I figure I should let them off the hook because I know going to the concert was a risky thing, and punishment was necessary. Losing the opportunity to say goodbye to Eddie will hurt me forever, but I deserve to be grounded.

"Mom, Dad I understand I can't go and why. I really messed up. May I have permission to call him long-distance to talk to him before he leaves? I know it costs money, but you can take the cost of the call out of my allowance. Please."

Dad talks this time since Mom is still crying, but so am I. He begins, "Emmy rules are rules."

I interrupt, "Yes, I know you have taught me that, I understand."

He starts again, "Please do not interrupt again."

"Yes sir, I won't."

He clears his throat and begins once more. "You're right, you broke a lot of rules, and punishing you is still our plan. But, we are revising our grounding. Today is the eighteenth of August, and you are grounded until the Friday before Labor Day. You will not be grounded that Friday, Saturday, Sunday, or Monday, which is Labor Day, *but* on Tuesday, you will finish your month of being grounded. So, I believe you have an invitation to a send-off party that weekend. I think this would be a good time to ask permission to go."

My mouth flew open, but nothing came out. I couldn't believe my ears. I can go. Oh, My God, I can go.

Dad looks at me puzzled and says, "Well?"

I burst out loudly, much louder than needed, "Mom, Dad, thank you for this amazing opportunity. May I have permission to go to the Miller's send-off party?"

I have the best parents in the world. I am so glad they work for stability in our world —they know what is important and what isn't.

I call Tootsie and tell her I can come, but I have serious rules to follow. "Most are simple. I can only be at your house or the party, unless, your parents are present. I cannot leave your house or the party with Eddie unless your parents are with me. You know the drill, no talking to strangers - etc well, well crap, you know the drill."

She laughs again and says, "This Podunk town, Hagerstown, Maryland, is not the big city. There's not so much excitement or trouble to get into here. You'll be fine."

There are ten young men drafted from our Senior Class of 1968 at St. Maria Goretti High School, and Eddie is just one of the ten. The party is for all of them. The military turned Tootsie's brother down, after they found out he has a heart condition. Sadly, it also ends his scholarship to play football in college. I am sure he is not taking *that* well. It has been his dream for *years*. Sean, one of the protection details attached to my dad, will take me to Tootsie's house Friday night and pick me up Monday afternoon.

With Mom and Dad gone again I am flanked by two bodyguards. At least they are considerate of my need for a little privacy. I think Mom and Dad are in Illinois at the Democratic National Convention or is it Cuba or both, I am not sure. They are in much better shape now and I am so glad.

THIRTY SIX

LANGLEY OPS

- Kitten is in Hagerstown, MD for the weekend. Her detail is headed by Sean since Big Bird and Whitey are still not one hundred percent.
- The other agents assigned there are locals who know the people involved.
- The Knights of Columbus and Miller residence both have been cleared.
- Kitten detail will be back to normal as soon as school is back in session on Tuesday.
- There is a notable addition to one rotating escort to John Hopkins University for a night class. New local agents are being assigned to Kitten for this detail.
- The schedule is available in packet.
- Tiger's detail is still in the works. She will be a freshman in one of the local high schools.
- Big Bird and Whitey will need the normal escort to Bethesda Naval Hospital for post-surgery check in.

THIRTY SEVEN

Say Goodbye

———◆———

THE PARTY IS SATURDAY, AND it is at the Knights of Columbus Hall in Hagerstown. Friday, Tootsie and I stay up all night talking. We decide to go shopping Saturday morning, then get ready for the party. I have brought clothes, but while shopping, I find The. Perfect. Dress. for the party. It is that perfect "little black dress".

All the fashion magazines are talking about having a go to dress that is black. I am fair skinned, but I have a decent tan this year. I can wear black and not look dead in it. I guess the tan is from the many days at the pool in Spain. So, this dress is a halter top which means no bra, then straight down to mid-thigh just grazing my hips is perfect.

Tootsie's eyes sparkle as she says, "Wow, Eddie will *love* that."

Tootsie is right, Eddie stares at me and smiles. Then his smile turns into a whisper in my ear, "I love the dress, but it is what's inside that turns me on. Watch out my sweet little girl."

Many of my friends ask me about Spain and my new school. Eddie never leaves my side, and he is holding my hand or has his arm around my waist. Wherever Eddie puts his hands on me, I am tingling. It is so distracting, but oh so nice. This is so much fun. Can this last forever?

Eddie keeps looking at me like he has something to say, but when I ask, he just says later when we are alone. My heart swells, and I want to leave right then. He is not ready to go, so we stay at the hall and dance and talk all evening, even though the official party ended around seven pm. I like this feeling I have for Eddie. I love him in a forever way, not just a short thrill. I am conflicted about Caesar. Not that I did anything with him, but that I might have, and then, I would regret that.

Being with Eddie tonight, I realize Caesar would have been a cheap thrill while Eddie is the real deal. I see a mature Eddie tonight, and I know it is the military influence. How much more will he change while he is away? All I can do is hope the changes will be small in the bad things and big in the good things. My head is spinning, time to be alone with him, please.

By nine pm Eddie says, "Let's go to Tootsie's."

I smile, no words needed. I wanted this to happen hours ago. I want him, and the time to be alone.

Bob and Tootsie's house is like Eddie's second home. He even has a key. The house is a very large place, and I have the guest house by the pool to myself. We walk quickly and quietly through the house and out to the small cottage by the pool. Everything is so quiet - well too quiet for the Miller's place.

The pool has a few lights on around it but not in the pool itself which gives the whole area a romantic glow. All the lawn chairs are in place and it is picture perfect. I think the house is way too quiet sort of spooky quiet. I am happy and like i's quietness and Eddie gives me a mischievous smile.

I say, "It's too quiet here, Eddie."

He says, "The Millers went from the party to Tootsie grandma's house in Pennsylvania. They will get back real late."

I am surprised and Eddie notices, as if he read my mind.

"I told Mr. and Mrs. Miller I would look after you."

I didn't want to think about what Sean would say if he knew there were no adults here, not to mention what my parents might do. Hmmmm, Sean seems to know all. Is he out there somewhere watching me or listening in? Do I care? Maybe, maybe not. I am excited, and maybe a little nervous. No, I am really nervous.

As we approach the cottage, I take off my shoes, put them on one of the lounge chairs, sit at the edge of the pool, and put my feet in. The water is still warm from the day's unseasonably warm weather. It feels so nice. Eddie follows me, but he is having a tough time rolling his jeans up so they won't get wet.

I tell him without hesitation," I think that is hopeless. If you don't want them wet, just take them off." Before I can finish my sentence, he has them off and is sitting by me. I turn my head to tell him there are extra swimsuits in the pool house, but no need. I swallow hard and say, "Nice boxers."

His smile is so much more than mischievous. It's downright steamy. I can't believe how crazy and brave I am because at that smile, I just slip into the pool dress and all. When I reemerge, I see the look on his face. Well, it is priceless, but now, I am scared to death. What have I just invited him to do?

In a heartbeat, he is standing in front of me in the water. Eddie has always been so careful with me. If I was twenty-six and he was twenty-eight then the age difference would be small but sixteen to eighteen feels like a big thing. If I said no, he Would have stopped. He always wanted to know how I feel. I love that about him. I am sure his emotions are running at high speed, and I have just encouraged him to go full steam ahead. I hate it when I hear girls talk about turning on a guy, and then putting the brakes on and say no. That will not be fair to him and could be dangerous. I know Eddie cares about me and respects me. Is this what I want cause this man in front of me is all in. I am not so sure. What do I say?

I guess Eddie really does know me well because he kisses me and pulls me close. I can *feel* what he wants. Yes, he is all in.

He pulls himself slightly away, looks me in the face, and says, "Yes?"

I hesitate, and he kisses me again.

"You aren't sure, are you?"

I still have no words — I just don't know how I feel. I think I love this man; I want to be intimate with him. He kisses me softly on the lips again and again with deeper need and we swim for a minute then he kisses me with an urgency that moved me to deepen the kiss. This deepened kiss is inviting him to do more.

"I am a virgin, and I want to stay that way for my wedding night. Call me old-fashioned or just a brain-washed Catholic girl, but that is how I feel in my *sane* moments. *This* isn't such a *sane* moment." I blurt all this out without a breath, not knowing what he will think.

Eddie pulls me close again, and his hands are slowly, carefully, lovingly, moving all over me. This feels so amazing. He moves both hands across my shoulders, and then over my nipples, which are now pressing through my dress. Then he moves down to my waist, and down, down, down to the hem of my dress. Eddie has such a gentle touch, but his eyes are on fire. He pauses and just breathes, looking deep inside me.

Eddie leans in and whispers, "I need you; I don't want to stop this." He whispers in my ear again, "I won't hurt you, and I will not push you. Will you trust me to satisfy both of our sexual needs *and* your emotional well-being? I need you now."

I step closer.

His eyes widen, and he lifts my dress over my head; we are skin-to-skin. I didn't even feel his boxers come off, I just feel his erection against me, and I shiver. He pulls me closer.

It is so hard to explain all the things racing through my brain. I want this, but not all the way. Can he stop? Would I want him to? Wait do I want this? Do I need protection? Can you get pregnant on the first time? Yes, I know you can, Does he? Does he care about that? Oh God, this is wonderful. I want to remember every moment.

We are standing in the pool; Eddie is naked, and I only have panties on, but they are next to go. He goes underwater and gently removes my panties. He reemerges with them, smiling.

His hands are surveying my body, again. He looks at me for a long time, and then mumbles, "Oh my God you are perfect" He steps up close again.

I can hardly stay in the moment. I love the feel of him pressing against my body. And, his hands are everywhere. I kiss him hard and long, then gently nibble on his neck.

He shivers, and let's out a moan, almost a growl, Then, the moment ends when he steps back and says, "shit,'. Then, he sees my expression of confusion "Oh shit, not your fault."

I am really confused.

He looks pissed. "I came, I am sorry."

Okay, I am so dumb because I'm still not sure what happened that made him so mad. I really never got the chance to get back to that moment because lights went on in the house. Double shit.

Within seconds, he is in the bathhouse and has a towel around him. I am inside the cottage door. I put on my swimsuit thinking, we might get to talk and swim together later. Having wet hair in a dry swimsuit is suspicious, but not as suspicious as being in the pool naked.

Of course, swimming later did not happen. Tootsie and her brother came outside to the pool. Tootsie is chattering away about the lights and why they aren't on when her brother gives Eddie a look that has a sneaky smile attached.

Finally, Tootsie stops dead, runs over to me, and says softly in my ear, "You had sex?" She looks at me, then at Eddie, and then back at me.

Eddie saves me. "Well, I might have if you hadn't interrupted. Thanks, little sis."

Tootsie is pissed, " I told you, Eddie — she wants to be a virgin when she gets married. What are you thinking? Are you crazy, or just dumb? Her dad is a really bad dude, and then there's her mom."

At this, I turn and walk into the cottage without saying a word. I am so embarrassed. They are talking about me like I am not there. And, my mom and dad are involved too. How uncool is that.

To Eddie's credit, he is on my heels and wants to talk. I let him. I listen, and we make each other feel right about the night. He wants me and I want him, but he also knows I do not want to go all the way. I am happy, but I need to be very intimate with him. I want his touch and kisses and I can hardly stay in the moment without his kisses. The lights go out on the first floor of the house.

"Everyone seems to have gone to bed," I say. I love this man. We spend the night together fulfilling each other's needs. He teaches me about orgasms. He is a patient teacher, and I am all in. At first, I was embarrassed, but Eddie takes it slow and makes learning such an amazing adventure into womanhood. Eddie is a sensual, wonderful man, He realizes my desire to be a virgin is important to me and respects that. I want him. In the morning, I am still a virgin. Well, I can hardly stay in the moment, technically, I guess.

I know he will be gone soon. My heart hopes he will return to me, on his journey in the military. I know he will meet many women along the way and they will be happy to fulfill all his physical needs. I have to hope he will not find someone to replace me, because I love this man. I will miss him. His tour of duty isn't going to be short enough to suit me.

The next morning, Tootsie comes bounding in the cottage to find us entwined in each other's arms. I did not move, but Eddie carefully makes sure I am covered and waves her out. She obeys without a word. I heard Tootsie's brother chastise her just outside the door.

Bob is lecturing Tootsie, "Eddie is a good guy, and if Emmy said no, he would respect that. Now, stop butting into Eddie's last time alone with her. Why don't you make a tray for them if you really feel you need to butt in. Try treating Emmy like an adult, not your little girlfriend. She looks like a full-fledged woman to me, and if Eddie didn't care so much for her, I would be standing in line."

Tootsie retorted, "She is like a sister to you. That's gross."

"Trust me, kid — she is a very attractive woman, and all of us guys are happy for Eddie. Now, go make a tray for your brother from another mother and your best friend."

Tootsie snorts but heads for the kitchen.

Bob sort of shouts at Tootsie's back, "I think next time you should knock before entering a bedroom, little sis."

Eddie rolls over, kisses me, and says, "Well, my full-fledged woman, I will have to be careful if the guys are standing in line, especially if Bob Miller is in that line."

I just smile, returning the kiss, and snuggling closer. I don't want to think about the goodbye kiss. Not yet.

Sunday and Monday are a blur. We swim together, play cards with everyone, doing just normal family stuff. We all are trying to ignore the elephant in the room. Eddie and the others will ship out early Tuesday morning. I was lucky enough to spend another intimate night with Eddie Sunday night. I want to do this every night for the rest of my life. Eddie is more than I ever dreamed about in a lover, and we haven't even "done it" all the way.

THIRTY-EIGHT

LANGLEY OPS

- Kitten in Hagerstown, Maryland. Surveillance is being coordinated by Sean
- Big Bird and Whitey and Tiger are at their residence

THIRTY-NINE

The Good and the Bad

MONDAY, SEAN ARRIVES WITH A gift from my parents for Eddie. It is a credit card to use to call me or his parents anytime he wants. I cry. This is it. I have to say good-bye. Eddie thanks Sean and says he will use it wisely. Then he says, "Sean, can you give us a minute or two before you take her away."

Sean says, "Sure, take your time."

We walk out to the cottage to get my things.

Eddie turns and says, "I will be back for you. I love you. I want to marry you, and I have ring here for you." He drops to one knee, "Will you marry, me Emerald Mist McCormick?"

I am dumbstruck. I practically jump into his arms. "Yes, of course."

Eddie kisses me and takes a deep breath.

Did he think I would say no?

"I haven't asked your dad for your hand in marriage because they are never home. He might be offended. I thought he might be here today. Tell him I am sorry. I hope he understands I couldn't leave without doing this. I need you. I want you. I love you." We kiss, I cry, he cries.

"Time to go." Eddie says and I see Tootsie and she is looking at my finger and then just dashes over to me and bear hugs me.

"Welcome to the family. I have a new sister," she announces.

Hugs and handshakes are given out.

Sean steps up and shakes Eddie's hand and says, "You're one lucky guy. My other thought is that you are a brave man to ask her without asking her Dad. But I think he will understand and be okay cause she is happy. Now her Mom well that's another story. Bring her flowers you might survive."

Everyone laughed. Tootsie took pictures and I kissed my man goodbye. I cried the whole way home, sometimes I smiled at my ring through. Two rings, two amazing men, I am so lucky.

FORTY

Langley OPS

- Kitten and Tiger are at the new house with Diane. Big Bird and Whitey will be back in twenty-four hours.
- Tiger is going to the local public school as a freshman. There are several retired military as teachers.
- We are vetting and will inform them of her status.
- Kitten will continue at a local Catholic high school for social time, attending college at night two days a week. Plus, she will dance, taping on Friday, and Saturday.
- Her security needs are complicated but low risk.
- Check your packets for assignments and more details.

FORTY ONE

New House, New School

IN OUR NEW HOME IN Timonium, Maryland, I am a little lost. Eddie writes he is shipping out to Germany and says he is excited to see Germany. What a relief he is not going to Vietnam, at least not yet. I am jealous I cannot explore Germany with Eddie. His letters make me want to run away to him.

I have thought of nothing else. But what is happening to him, and where are they sending him? My thoughts constantly linger on where Eddie is and what is he doing. I have to struggle to not let my loss of Eddie take over my day-to-day life. It is weird being engaged and seventeen. I don't have anyone to talk to about being engaged here. I am not going to talk about it with these new friends. I wouldn't even know how to start a conversation. I could say, "Hi, Nice to meet you. Go to a party? Oh, by the way, I am engaged." That wouldn't work. I will have to be satisfied with talking to Tootsie when I can. She is still in high school too and not so happy I didn't tell her I had graduated with her brother. I think if I had, we could have made that journey of graduating early together or at least tried. She is also very smart.

I guess my choices with teenage girls is not on track yet. Spain is a pleasant, confusing memory, but college seems to be for old people. So, what am I to do here besides dance and write to Eddie?

My mom has convinced me to go back to high school just for fun and social time. She thinks high school will suit me better this time around, and I can ease into college life by taking a class at night. Yeah, I know —fun no pressure, just fun. I guess parents look back and think of high school as fun with no problems. I like school, and the academic part is a piece of cake, but socially, yikes, it is scary for me. Well, it appears everyone thinks I need the practice with kids my age. Hmmm, maybe I don't, because I am an engaged woman now. I am sure this anxiety will lessen as I get out and go with the flow of life. I mean no more bombs or boarding school just normal everyday teenage life, right? But also, sadly, no more Eddie. I need something to do, because I miss Eddie so much. I write, but really, I want to climb in the envelope and be mailed to him.

Fitting into this new high school is important to me, I really want to fit in I want to be in the moment. I soon realize most people here have gone to school together all their lives, like I had at Saint Maria Goretti. This isn't going to be easy. Maybe I should have chosen the high school on base, at least I would know someone there. Maybe Tootsie's parents can adopt me, and I could stay there. Yikes, no, then, I would have to face all those kids who know me and Archie and Eddie. Not good at all. Besides, the Miller's are moving to California. I will miss talking and being with Tootsie and her family. I wonder why long-distance calls are so expensive. Oh well, more letters to write, so we won't lose touch. I have learned to like meeting new people ever since my experience with Caroline and Archie.

Oh, Eddie, I miss you.

His words from his latest letter fill my head. He says, "You can do this and like it. You are bound to a life, meeting new and interesting people. Take a deep breath, you have lived in your parents' world, where you meet many new adults all the time. This new high school is no different."

Caroline's words are floating there too, "Emmy, you are good with new people. You just don't know it."

Thinking of them reminds me of how lucky I am to have friends like Eddie and Caroline in my head to help me forward. I now know I come from a different kind of life from most kids. What happens if these kids notice I am different? I mean it isn't written on my forehead but it must show someway in my speech or look because I feel like they know. In the past I have been lucky that

I have not been bullied because I am different. Will I get bullied here? Different doesn't work well in high school college yes, high school no. I am accustomed and comfortable to talking to adults.

Okay so, I am not weird, wel, l maybe just different. But my life schedule is weird. I go to high school in the morning and take all art classes and go to John Hopkins University a couple nights a week. Then, on Fridays, hop a train with a handler in tow to Philadelphia to tape "American Bandstand". I would love to have shared my world, but that just isn't happening, at least not yet, not in person anyway. I think that would take too much explanation. And, who would I tell I don't know anyone well enough. And besides, who would even care. My first week at school, I try to chat with any and all the friendly smiles I can find. This is not as hard as I thought it would be. Thank God.

One very intuitive girl, Sarah, asks me to sit with her and her friends at lunch. So, I do, she is nice and straightforward. As she explains, her group is the B group you know, the non-cheerleaders, non-dance team, or super athletics. Those members are the A group. This is so crazy. She has this down to a science. I love it.

Sarah lowers her voice, "You are pretty enough for the A group, and smart enough too."

"What?" is all I can muster. What does that mean?

Sarah continues by leaning in more.

"I have seen you practice for cheerleading try-outs, and I think you have a good chance. But, if you make it, you will knock out one of the A group girls. The A group girls will not like that, and then, they will not accept you. They can tell you have talent and are worried."

I am stunned, and now a little worried too. I don't want to make a nemesis. "How do you know this?"

She explains, I have childhood friends who are part of the A group, and of course, the B group. "I am not pretty enough to be totally accepted by all the pretty ones, and I am way too nice so I am not a threat."

I am stunned again. Could all this be true? It kind of gave me the creeps. She seems to think I will fall into the same situation half in half out.

She says, "I feel sorry for you.".

I am really worried now. I never noticed the groups at my other high school. I will have to ask Tootsie. I was a cheerleader there, but not an athlete. I never really tried any sports. I was in the Theatre group.

I told Sarah this, and she laughed again. See one foot in each group. This really makes me wonder and sends me to my mom.

My mom listens. Then, she laughs and laughs and laughs. We try to brainstorm a solution. I ask her why she laughed. Resigned, Mom sighed. "High school never changes, and it is a shame. I don't have a solution, but I have an idea that might enlighten a few of the kids who have true hearts."

My mom's heart is true, sometimes rough, but clear, thoughtful, and true. How lucky I am.

I tell Mom, "I am so glad to have you as a friend."

She looks at me with her strong, firm eyes and says, "I am your mom first, and maybe, when you are eighteen, we can be friends. I hope we will be friends, but right now, you need me to be Mom, not your friend."

I am so confused by this, but I trust her.

We planned a party to die for. Long story short, it took three totally cool parties to satisfy the gossips of the groups. All the parties are fun, I make friends, and the gossips shut up about the new kid. My mom is amazing, and again, I realize how lucky I am. I plan to be just like her when I have kids. I hope.

I do have lots of "surface friends"-you know friends who are not candidates to be forever friends — after these parties, but I really only find two girls I think are worth my time to befriend as best friends. Well, plus Sarah. Mary Margaret Wilson and Harriett (Bunny) Brownyeah, I know, Bunny Brown. That name also kind of scares me too. I think it sounds like a stripper name, but I will never tell her I think that.

Mary Margaret is a stately beauty with blue-black hair that tumbles down her back in ringlets, and she is a nerd. Okay, you guessed it; I am a nerd too. So, we get along great. If you can hide being a nerd, you can survive high school - I already knew that. With Mary Margaret, I don't have to hide my neediness, but she does not understand my love of dancing and painting and cheerleading. She often wonders why I do not just rely on my brain power alone. She doesn't belong to either group And I think she likes it that way. But I know she is lonely. I am proved right when the first boy who pays any attention to her gets her pregnant. Yikes, that is scary.

Mary Margaret says it was just one time. She is lucky because this boy, well older guy, seems to love her, and wants to marry her and raise their child. She decides to marry him, makes plans to test out of high school, and go to college early. She has her daughter and joins the adult world of parenting. I miss her. If Eddie were here, I could be her. Is that what I want? Does he want that? I haven't heard any hint of kids in his letters. I think I will try to talk to him. How does he feel about kids?

With Mary Margaret gone the beautiful spring days seem to have a dark cloud hanging over me. I try to talk to Bunny about Mary Margaret but she doesn't see Mary Margaret at all. Mary Margaret is not in the A group or B group, so she doesn't exist in Bunny's mind.

Sarah is around, and I hang out with her when I need a reality check. She is always with a group, sometimes the A group, sometimes the B group. I think the B group is more fun, nicer to talk to, and easier to be with. I think this is her security blanket, and she is nothing but understanding with me. Still she is one of the biggest gossips, and nothing is sacred in her eyes. As much as I am grateful for her friendship, I have not told her about Eddie. I want him to myself for now, even if he is not here in person. I am pretty sure if she knew about him, everyone else would too.

FORTY-TWO

LANGLEY OPS

- Kitten's new friends Harriett A Brown, Mary Margaret Wilson, Sarah L Carrollton, need to be vetted, along with the entire cheerleading squad.
- The boyfriend, Lysinger, is still in Germany for now, check on status and report back.
- Agents assigned to Kitten need to vet social events not only for security but also for suitability.

FORTY-THREE

The First Time

BUNNY IS FROM THE A group, but she does travel with the B group when she needs an ego stroke. She is fun and is not a gossip, but she is Number One. If you understand that your wishes are *always after* her wishes, then you could be her friend. Well, I begin to trust her and love to hang out. The boys love her pouty lips, turned up nose, and her freckles—kind of like a beautiful Kewpie doll. And, she is just fun.

I just have one problem with Bunny — she never really believes my home life. I think she thinks I am inventing it. This keeps me from sharing Eddie with her. Bunny's parents are accountants at home, and they never leave the house and I mean never. They have everything delivered — food and everything. It seems creepy. But who am I to judge. My life is different too.

There is finally a moment that makes Bunny sort of understand when a group of us go to a big dance at school, she spots the bodyguard following us that night to the restaurant, then to the dance, and later. I truly treasured the moment when I could say, "I told you".

To my amazement, she finally takes the time to watch "Soul Train" and sees me dancing. But, even then, she says she thinks it could be someone who just looks a lot like me. I have her give me one of her many beautiful pins, and I wear it on set, so she can see it and know it is really me. This did the trick, and it is such a relief to finally have someone in my new high school that sees a little of my real life, even though it's not much, not all.

My mom is right - high school is a lesson in survival. For most of the average students, a high school diploma should say I survived the crazy social stuff, the teachers who make you jump through unnecessary academic hoops within a specific time frame, and pass generic tests to satisfy the state legislators. All we really show is we can regurgitate information. No critical thinking or problem solving. My first high school had a total of about 200 students, and my second high school has 400 students. So, everyone still knows everyone else. Is this good or bad? I am not sure.

By January 1970, I finally have a solid routine. High school in the mornings, and college in the afternoon, evenings. It is a busy time. Mom and Dad are in South America again, Peru, Chile, and Ecuador. My parents were in Chile when I was born, so my guess they use that as sort of "home base" there.

I finally am resigned to having a handler with me at all times and why I need to have one. I am pretty sure it's because Mom and Dad's job, where they deal with sensitive, international issues. Of course, I don't know the details. But, when they talk privately, I try to eavesdrop, so I am not always in the dark. I am confused by the talk of Nazis. History tells me all that nonsense ended with World War II, but not for them. I know Castro and Cuba are not a place for Americans, but my parents talk about being there, that worries me. What do they do with Castro and then Nazis I can't imagine. I tried looking both up at the school library, but that effort got me nowhere. I guess I will have to remember to watch the eleven o'clock news and see if that helps.

Going to college in the afternoon/evening at the beautiful John Hopkins University in Baltimore is so fun, and I love going there. I am enrolled in some intro classes in painting, so I have studio time. I have always loved to paint and draw and just doodle. But, at college, I am being guided to bigger and better, skills in all of those processes.

Studio time happens once a week and gets out after dark. It is really spooky around campus with all the big trees and the shadows they create. The trees are old and tall and loom above you. I'm not worried cause one of the handlers' is always at the door and walks with me to the car. It is late April, Truly a beautiful evening.

John Hopkins is an old campus with lovely big trees and long pathways to the parking lots. The trees are just beginning to come to life after a long winter. The pathway from the studio building to the parking lot spans down the side of the huge three-story Fine Arts building winding around trees and park benches as it goes. I love the peaceful feeling of the campus at night but one evening things go horribly wrong.

Class is over, and I am so excited. I have turned in my first college portfolio, so I have a sense of accomplishment and the satisfaction of finishing my first art class at a college level. I am exhilarated. It is in the 50's, and a clear night with a slight breeze that make the trees gently rustle. It is definitely still "Sweater Weather", so for April, it is chilly.

My handler is not right at the door, like he always is. Hmmmm, maybe I just don't see him. I'm not too worried, and I am still thinking of my huge accomplishment. I feel like I am glowing and wish my parents were home, so I could share my excitement with them. I start to walk towards where he usually parks. I look down at my watch, and as I look up, I see him. I raise my hand to wave at my handler as something or someone jumps on me from a hedge to my right. We hit the ground and begin to roll down the grassy slope. Thank God, I hit the grass and not the concrete.

Who is this? Which one of my friends thinks this is funny? But this is not a friend because this man is grabbing at me and pulling me close to him, it is not romantic. There *is* an intimacy about this grip he has on me. There is a familiar smell to him too. Is it his cologne? Where do I know this smell from?

I am confused. He is pulling me into him, like a protective cocoon, but I am pushing away. The familiar smell, and then when he speaks, the familiar voice does not go with what is happening.

Then, fear took over. Oh my God! Is he trying to rape me? I need help. Okay Emmy, slow down, get you head together, you can do this. We are rolling faster now. I give myself a mental slap —I need to fight or surrender. But surrender is not an option for me, so I kick and scream. He is strong, and he is hanging on, talking to me. I am not going to listen. I don't want to listen. Wait, is he talking to me in Spanish? Yes, he is talking to me in Spanish. Sweet soothing, sounding words. God, why hadn't I learned more in Spain. He is familiar, but why? He is not going to sweet talk me. I decide to fight harder, and I am going to give it my all. Kicking, screaming, and trying to swing my arms as we plummet down the cold, wet, grassy hill is my only plan to get away. If we stop, maybe I can knee him. That should buy me some time to get away. Where is my handler?

Finally, I catch a phrase in English that stops me cold and makes me listen.

"I told you I would see you again, Kitten, I am here."

"What?" I start fighting and pushing away as we roll to a stop.

I try to see who this is. The hoodie has his face covered. I need to move away from him to see him better. I guess he decides he doesn't need my cooperation, so he punches me in the mouth, and my lights go out.

FORTY FOUR

Langley OPS

- Kitten was compromised last night.
- Joe was seriously hurt but will recover good as new in time. The perp got away but without Kitten thanks to Joe.
- Kitten is also in the hospital for a day or two and after some dental work she will be ok.
- Big Bird and Whitey are still in Germany but will make a call to check on Kitten when she can talk.
- These assets are concerned about our security detail with Kitten.

FORTY FIVE

Another Hospital Visit

WHEN MY LIGHTS CAME BACK on, I am definitely no longer on the grass at Johns Hopkins. Instead, I am in a hospital again. My parents are not in the country, so there is one of my handlers, but it's not the one who came to pick me up. Dean and Diane are standing over me. My face is numb, and I hurt all over.

"Ow I hurt," I say to no one in particular.

In a straightforward manner, Diane softly explains, "Two broken ribs, a black eye, a broken arm, and just pain will do that. Oh yeah and you are missing a tooth."

I reach up to touch my mouth and realize I am tethered to an IV. I cry.

Dean explains, "Joe saw it happen and ran to stop it. He did it because it is his job, but it came at a cost. Joe arrived to see the man lying on top of you and talking to you."

Dean looks serious and then asks, "Did you know your attacker? What was he saying to you?"

I look up and say, "I know he talked to me, but it was mostly in Spanish."

The food tray arrived with a tall glass of pink stuff that looked like a strawberry shake. It did have a strawberry flavor, but it is blended with proteins and vitamins. I tried this strawberry-blended drink, and it is tasty, but all I want is a cheeseburger and fries.

The nurse just smiles and says, "It will be another twenty-four hours before you can have solid food."

The smell of good food wafts in from the hall when I start to tell Dean about the familiar smell and what I remembered he said.

I tell him, "It just doesn't make sense. I think he knew me, so I must have known him.

He asks me, "Was it Caesar?"

Was it Caesar? Maybe, I am not sure, and I said so.

In the fight that had ensued, Joe was stabbed, and he is also here at Bethesda Naval Hospital with me but in a different wing. The man escaped but seriously injured Joe in the process. Joe, I am told will be okay, but he will need time to heal. I wish I knew who it was. I think, it could it have been Carlos or Caesar? Maybe… so confusing.

I say, "I think I will have a clearer memory when the pain meds stop."

I am just glad I am still alive, and Joe will be Okay. I learn a life lesson that I am definitely glad to have a handler nearby. After some investigation, the man was not an American. Was I in the wrong place wrong time? No, it was something else. It sure freaked my parents out. They talked to me on the phone—well, they talked, I listened because my face hurt. I have to have a false tooth put in. The tooth that was knocked out is right in the front, and my busted lip is many colors. I am glad they can't see me. I am glad Eddie can't see me either. I am glad I don't have to go to school. I am a mess, and I just hurt all over.

When the bomb went off in our driveway and I went to boarding school, I learned that was a direct result of my dad and Mom being part of negotiating team dealing with "The Bay of Pigs" and the "Cuban Missile Crisis". Now, I wonder what my parents are up to that would cause someone to come after *me*. I am secretly wishing this is a "in the wrong place, wrong time thing", and not Caesar, and not because of my parents, but I seriously doubt it.

When Diane and Dean take me home, I try to get them to talk, but that's not working. I decide to just tell them what I think is happening in hopes they will agree or not. At least, then, I will have *some* info. I begin with, "I know Mom and Dad are in South America and Europe a lot these days. I think Frankfurt, Germany is one of their stops while in Europe because the Nuremberg trials are ongoing. Dad speaks fluid German, just like a native. He might be an interpreter.

Diane says, "He is more involved than that. That sparks my interest, but Diane clams up. Dean glowers at her, and neither will answer any more questions, I think she has screwed up by telling me that much. I'll try that again later.

The pain killers from the hospital make me dream. I keep dreaming about Caesar, and that makes me blush when I think about it the next morning. That evening in the alley is playing over and over in my head, like it is on a loop. I can't shake the feeling I am missing something. I really want to dream about Eddie. When I wake up, I chide myself each time for dreaming of Caesar and not Eddie. I haven't gotten a letter in a week. This makes me worry. I am also worried they will ship me to the wilderness after this attack at John Hopkins University but thankfully they don't.

FORTY-SIX

LANGLEY OPS

- Status on Joe, he is improving and is estimated to be back on office duty in a month.
- Kitten will be okay after the holidays to return to school but for now she will be restricted to home.
- Caesar Castillo and Carlos Ramos have been seen leaving US through Canadian border in New York two days after assault.
- Both seemed injured in the photos.
- There is a team working that angle.

FORTY-SEVEN

Cuban Girls

THIS ATTACK SEEMS SO SENSELESS and unnecessary to injure kids because of other things adults are up to in the world. Why hurt kids? It makes me remember when Dad brought the two young girls out of Cuba to be "my sisters" and they become my new roommates at the boarding school. Lucy and I had only been there three months.

He seems to *need* to protect these girls just as he does us. They lived in a place of unrest while we lived in a very sheltered environment. Still, bad things can and do happen here. When Elena and Ida Bustamante arrive, they are scared and speak only a little English.Dad arrived late at night, and the Mother Superior calls Lucy and I to the front foyer. We are in our pajamas. I just can't believe Mother Superior thinks it was okay to stay in our pajamas, but we do. Normally, we would need to be in dress uniforms to come to the front lobby. You could tell Dad is glad to be home. He hugs us so hard I think I might break in half. As Dad hugs me, I could see the two girls have sad eyes, and wait, tears too.

Dad says, "Make these girls your sisters, share your clothes, and everything until their things arrive."

They are dirty and look like their hair had not been washed in days.

Mother Superior says, "Take them to get a bath and pajamas and I will have food bought up."

Lucy and I kiss Dad goodbye, and we promise to take care of

Elena and Ida.

Elena is younger than Lucy and has golden-blonde hair braided down her back. She is as tall as I am and fair-skinned. Ida is in between Lucy and me in age, but she is closer to Lucy's height, at five-foot-five. She is stocky with dark-tanned skin and dark, black hair to the shoulders. I know their real names might be different, but at the time, Lucy and I just needed to take care of them.

Later, I discover "Bustamante" is their mother's maiden name, their last name is really Baptista. Yep, no wonder they were terrified. Dad said they had seen many of their family killed. I saw bad things on the news, but this was too close.

Elena and Ida stayed at the boarding school for three years, so did Lucy. They became great friends. FAV was founded in 1846 and had been a school since 1823. But its name was different then. There are "boarders" and day students, but all girls. The nuns are cloistered. If you don't know what that means, it means the nuns don't leave the property. It is approximately twelve spacious acres but still to never leave the property? That's crazy, but true.

I think this is a really crazy thing, so Ida and I decide to test it well, I decide, and Ida goes along with it. We go out the back gate to get some ice cream at the store down the street. it sounds like a perfect idea. Right? We can leave and they can't.Well, that did not work out so great. I didn't know there were "out sisters". I learned later there is a small group of sisters who can leave the property whenever it is necessary. One chased us. Boy can she run, even in her habit. Sister Baptista was five-foot four, rotund lady, about two hundred and fifty pounds. She seemed as round as she was tall. I look back to see her grab her long skirt with one hand and start running after us. Ida freaked out, and I had to pull her along, so it slowed me down. I was sure we could out-run her. But I soon learned she was fast, really fast. Needless to say, she caught us. She grabbed me by the scruff of my collar, pulling me to a stop. She looked me in the face and smiled so sweetly.

Her words were sugary-sweet as she explained, "You will be sweeping out the big ovens in the sisters' kitchen for *days*." The convent baked the best bread and rolls I have ever eaten, and now, I would learn where. I had to clean the ovens for a week. It was hard work.

I laughed out loud. When Dean approached quickly my daydream was over and I realized I was back to the scary hospital. Dean asks" What's up?"

"Sorry. Had a flash back." Dean looks my way, "About your attacker?" No just girl stuff. Dean stays close until Mom and Dad got home two days later. I think I am becoming a real pain and problem for my parents.

I learn during this high school time, I like and trust my parents, and even myself. I am looking forward to disappearing into a college far, far away from this group of dysfunctional, highly-motivated kids. I also learn I am naive and sheltered and protected. I feel privileged my parents could do this for me, so I filed away that thought. I hoped when I have kids, I can give them the same privileges I have and I can let my kids be kids for a long time, or as long as they need it. Tricky wish, but I could hope. I also wish my future kids would appreciate it, as I am beginning to of my parents.

My summer of 1970 is a quiet summer. I need that. I spend that summer packing my clothes for college in the fall and writing to Eddie. His letters are erratic in length and delivery. Something is changing, and I can't get him to talk about it.

FORTY EIGHT

Langley OPS

- The Houston team will take over the Kitten detail after a week or so.
- Tiger's DETAIL will stay the same.
- Diane will stay with Tiger until the new agent is intelled in.
- Big Bird and Whitey will take Kitten to college, and then they will go back to work from Houston.

FORTY NINE

College

IT IS THE FALL OF 1970, and I am on my way to a four-year college away from home finally. I am given choices as to colleges, but NO colleges in capital cities. Suggested states were Utah, Montana, Arkansas, and Texas. All the of them were too cold, except Texas. This new adventure has me worrying a lot. I will be alone in a state where I don't know a soul. I have a lot of worries and questions and no one I trust not to laugh at me who I could talk to.

I would like to have had a conversation with my mom about sex, but she was born in 1919, and I am sure she really doesn't have a clue where to begin. I guess I really don't need a sex talk since Eddie is so far away, and he can teach me whatever I need to know when he comes home. I know I will meet many attractive men here in Texas, and Eddie will meet many women there in Germany — we have talked about it in our letters. I have told him to come home to me, but I know he needs fun too. I do worry about him finding someone else who is more adult-like and not like this naive girl, but I am trying trust his true heart is mine.

My parents drive me to college. Yeah, I know all the way to Houston, Texas from Washington, DC. I thought they would hang out for a day or so, but nope, they hopped a flight to Puerto Rico to meet up with friends or so they said. I mean, they got me moved into the dorms called Moody Towers, and then, they kissed me bye and were gone.

Time to grow up and walk forward as a quasi-adult. So, I am

excited to be here alone, unchaperoned every minute, and I am scaredno terrified. I wish Eddie was here.

I know the academic work is a cakewalk for me but the rest is like being on another planet. My planet is "Planet Houston". The University of Houston in 1970 is a situated on the edge of the Third Ward near Texas Southern University, and according to the paper and TV, the racial unrest of this summer is still surging onto the U of H main campus. I am warned to be cautious, but to me, it is no scarier than my past experiences. Mom and Dad said I would soon meet the handlers who would check in on me, so I just try to keep my eyes open for them and trouble.

My first walk across campus to the Hofheinz Pavilion, the basketball arena, is for the cheerleader, Cougar Dolls and Houston Honey tryouts, and it is organized by the dorm staff. My dorms, "The Moody Towers" are new and on the opposite side of the campus from the athletic facility. The dorm rep, five other girls, and I start out with plenty of time to get there.

A fast walk would take fifteen minutes, but we left forty five minutes early with a planned stop to meet up with two girls at the other dorms, the Quadrangle, "The Quad" as everyone here calls it. I appreciate the effort to walk us to tryouts together. I researched a little about Texas before I came here and found out it is called, "The Friendly State". The longer I am in Texas, the more I have found they are friendly, and it is a called that for good reason - most people here are just that friendly.

The Quad is just four stories high, while the "Towers" are eighteen stories. Both dorms are surrounded by a stand of beautiful, old oak trees. We arrive at the Quad and decide to wait on a bench nestled in these Oaks until the other girls come out.

The sun is thankfully having a hard time peering through the branches of these beautiful, old oaks. It is remarkably cool in the shade, almost like a cool, summer night. Where the sun does penetrate, there are these stunning beams of light. I sit there waiting on the others, lost in my thoughts, remembering a poem/lullaby that I love by Meredith Willson. "I see the moon, and the moon sees me; The moon sees somebody I want to see. I see the moon and the moon sees me Under the shade of the old oak tree.

Please let the light that shines on me shine on the one I love. Over the mountains, over the sea, back where my heart is longing to be, please let the light that shines on me shine on the one I love."

Whoa, wait, where did that come from? I usually, whether in a dream or awake, think of that poem when I am afraid for a family member or a friend. Something scary or bad would have just happened or worse is about to.

I look up to see I am being talked to. Everyone is staring at me and is ready to go. I have to learn to stay in the moment, or I am going to fall into looking like that weird person my mom has warned me about becoming. Lots of times smart people are in their own world, and they tend to miss what is going on around them. Therefore, they alienate others when they don't seem interested. "Careful Emmy!" I apologize for daydreaming, and off we go.

Loud noises break the peacefulness of these beautiful, ancient trees. Everyone stops dead when we realize someone is screaming in pain. We see the road through the trees ahead of us, and we can also see a large group of people marching in the middle of the four lanes of traffic on Cullen Blvd. The group isn't like the marches I have seen in Washington, DC — these people are angry. I feel like I am watching a swarm of angry bees. The object of their anger is aimed at a tall, white kid. His blond hair really sticks out amongst the all-black crowd. I wonder what he did.

I realize I have slipped into a daydream again or am just hypnotized by what I am seeing when the organizer of the group, Cindy grabs my arm and pulls me down. "Stay down. You are the wrong color to be out here right now."

I give her a seriously crazy look.

"I'm black if you hadn't noticed and you are white. Stay down."

So, I did. I sit down close to the largest oak and a big azalea bush with beautiful, white flowers to watch. It is awful.

In front of me, I can see the blonde being swallowed up by the crowd. I look hard for him in the group, and then, there he is on the ground. He needs help. My heart says, "Go help, "but my brain says, "Too dangerous." The decision is made for me when the sirens go off. I am not sure what happened, or who called the police, but that sound —for me —is a relief.

The crowd in the street dissipates as if a bomb went off in its center. They are all gone within seconds. Some even blew by us hiding in the bushes. When I chance a look, all I can see is the kid on the ground in the street with a red flower blooming from his chest. He is not moving, but I am. I arrive at his limp body a second or two before a well-dressed man does.

He is my handler, and he touches my arm and says very quietly, "Stand up, and walk away, Emmy."

I look up at this man who has to be there for me and say, "I can't just walk away."

His soft, smooth voice comes back with words that make me come back to the moment. "Help is near, and this could cause you to be extracted."

My new friends arrive. Well, I feel them arrive, but no one speaks.

My handler says, "Go on to the tryouts it is safe, there."

Cindy grabs me and helps me up, "That guy is gone. We can't help him anymore."

As we walk away, Cindy looks back peppering me with a ton of questions.»Who is that? It seemed like he knows you. Is he your brother? Your boyfriend? He's kind of old for you. Didn't think you would go for an old guy."

I just stare at her.

Tryouts are a blur. Everyone is talking about two things—the riot and the stabbing. I am not just quiet but silent. I feel like a robot. I do as I am told just like I always do. What is this world coming to? I am dancing, and a real person just died. For what?

I guess Cindy realized I am in shock because she guided me around to all three groups. The cheerleaders are for football and basketball, The Houston Honeys the dance team are for basketball. The Cougar Dolls the dance team are for the football team, and all had different check in points. Most are not trying out for all three, but I am. We arrived about eight thirty in the morning, and finish around three in the afternoon. I think I ate lunch, but who knows. They will post a list at both dorms.

I just want to eat and to go home. I want to know about the blond kid. What could he have done that warranted a death sentence? I guess I am used to my mom and dad in scary situations, but I never thought about people on the street being in real danger. By the time I am ready to leave, almost everyone is gone but Cindy. Now I look at her, and for the first time, I really notice that she is black and really pretty.

She looks as tired as I feel. "Come on, let's go get something to eat, and then go back to dorms and just fall in bed."

I nod. I am hungry, and don't care what we eat.

As we walk outside, I can see my life is about to wrap Cindy into it whether she wants that or not, and I'm not sure how she will react. My handler is standing in front of a large car and beckons me to it. I don't even know his name. I go up to him and explain Cindy and I are on our way to go eat, then back to the dorms.

He says, "Okay, I will drive you anywhere you want."

I explain, I was planning on eating at the dorm since I do not have much money with me. I do not know where to get food close by. The cafeteria at the dorm doesn't open until six pm and that is two and half hours from now.

"Will you take us two places — the dorms for money and then to get food? I owe Cindy. She took good care of me today."

He smiles big and says, "I can do better than that."

To my delight, he takes us to the "Spaghetti Warehouse" in downtown Houston. This Italian restaurant is a really different-looking place. Some of the tables are in engulfed inside a bed frame so you seem to be eating in bed. The antiques and vintage collections on the walls are fun to look at.

My handler now has a name, Mark, and he explains, "I need to first call your Dad with a personal update on your state of mind."

I plead with Mark, "Please do not worry my parents too much."

He nods and disappears for a moment.

I didn't have to explain a thing to Cindy. She just went with it.

Cindy is so nice and is very intrigued by his actions. I could tell she did want to know what was going on but was too polite to ask. I don't even know where to begin to explain. when Pete came back he did explain to Cindy and took the time to help her understand what was up and the need for discretion. I vowed to use his explanation in the future. What he said to her was all true and I didn't sound so weird the way he explained it. She smiled and reassured him she could abide by his suggestions. Cindy is already on the Houston Honeys dance team, but she has to re-audition each year. I am invited to the callback for all three teams. There are five of us who are invited to all three. Callbacks are in two days, but it will be a very long wait.

    Cindy says she will walk with me again. I am happy about that. The idea of going alone makes my skin crawl. I know I can ask to be driven, but I am working on independence and normalcy.

FIFTY

LANGLEY OPS

- Houston seems to still be a hot box for civil unrest. and Kitten got caught up in it today.
- Mark IS there as a temporary handler, and things worked out as well as could be expected.
- She may need a little more security until things settle down. We are considering options.
- Sean is still on the ground there, and he will stay longer to make sure everything is in place.
- There are no other issues with other family members.

FIFTY-ONE

Fitting In

RACIAL UNREST IN HOUSTON TOOK a step back for a while with all the publicity, but things soon settled down after all the media frenzy. I am very happy about this.

The dance and cheerleading tryouts are a lot of work, but it's my passion, so I loved it. I find out I am not a dancer for the football field. I can high kick, but over and over and over again in a line is not for me. The Houston Honeys are more dancing, and less 'spectacle', so I did so much better at this.

The cheerleading sponsor is also one of the gymnastic coaches, so she knows what I am capable of. Hence. cheerleading went well too. Slowly, the University of Houston is turning out to be my safe haven, even though it started out badly.

Much to my delight, I am now a Houston Honey and the Cougar mascot. I am scheduled for just twelve hours of class time, so I know I can easily fit rehearsal into my academic schedule.

My days are full, but I love this. Cindy is in a sorority so her social life revolves around it. She said I would make a great AKA, Alpha Kappa Alpha, but that could never happen. This is very confusing I thought she likes me. My dad had been a Sigma Chi at Columbia University so I am a legacy whatever that is. I wonder why I cannot be an AKA. Sometime, when I work up the courage to ask why, I will.

Cindy and I meet in between classes for lunch sometimes. Our meeting place this time is at the University Center, or UC as we call it. It is three stories with a courtyard in the middle. The middle floor has the bookstore and offices for student organizations. The top floor is more offices and study areas. Comfy sofas and tables to work quietly. On the bottom floor is the Cougar Den, which is a meeting place and dining area. At any time, night or day, you can find groups there eating, playing cards, or generally hanging out.

At a lunch break with Cindy, down in the Cougar Den, I ask, "Hey you know everything about sororities and fraternities. What is a legacy?"

Her head jerks around, "Are you one?"

I answer, "Yes, whatever that means."

Cindy laughs, "You will know soon. Oh, and it's not bad."

Thirty seconds later, Cindy stands, climbs up on her chair, and shouts in a southern accent she does not have, "Hey Cougar Den, I need me a white sorority chick. I got me a legacy here who needs info."

Three very put-together, beautiful women materialize out of thin air. I am stunned. They are not only beautiful, but the epitome of the perfect sorority girl. Cindy says her hellos and goodbyes, then excuses herself to her next class. I don't have a class until practice time.

As Cindy starts to leave, she says, "See you at practice." I give her a thumbs up.

She nods and jogs off to class.

"Hi," says the tall blonde standing directly in front of me, "I'm Susan McCoy, I am a Delta Gamma." Susan points to the next girl, a brunette with a pixie haircut. She is the shortest of the three and the hair cut must be new because she keeps touching the cute curl in front off her ears. "This is Megan Plummer. She's an Alpha Chi Omega." I nod and so does she. The third girl is very tall with the most luxurious long ringlets cascading down to mid back. She is the tallest of the three and as she moves so do all those ringlets. "And, that's Carol Anne Landry, and she is a ZETA." I must look like a deer in the headlights. Susan continues, "I understand you are a legacy?"

I came back to life, and I realize, at that moment, I need to use all my social know-how with these beautiful social butterflies. My mother always says, "Head up, shoulders back, look the problem straight in the eye, smile, and believe people want to be good." This will be fun, but it will also test me.

I perk up and say," Yes, I believe I am, but I have no idea how that works. Can one of you enlighten me? I will be ever so grateful."

At that, Carol Anne smiles back and says," Well then, let's get down to business. May we sit?"

I nod, and they do. I am surrounded by three confident-looking women. One blonde and two brunettes. They could have just been peeled from a fashion magazine. I am not dressed like they are, but I am in a stylish peasant blouse and jeans. Still, I feel under-dressed sitting with these women. Again, I feel like the little sheltered kid with no idea how to dress myself.

Carol Ann continued, "Why do you think you are a legacy ? The registrar usually appraises us if a new student has a fraternity background, so we can invite them to a rush party."

Megan, the little pixie girl, chirps in. "The system isn't perfect, but between that and the survey all freshmen fill out, it seems to work. I don't know how you slipped through."

I reply, "Could be that happened because I did not make my final decision to come here until eight days ago."

Megan says, "Well, that would do it."

Susan takes over the conversation again and asks a barrage of questions. I like this straight-forward approach. Of course, this seems to make the other two a little uncomfortable. "So, what's your name? Where are you from? You don't have much of an accent. Are you a freshman? What are you in to? What practice do you have with Cindy? How did you meet Cindy? Where do you live? Do you have a car?" Susan wasted no time, and I like that.

Ok where to begin without bragging or giving too much info to these girls whom I don't know but enough to spark their interest.

Hmmm, what do I know about them? I know I should tailor this to each of them. This will get them wanting more. I am not a national champion at extemporaneous speaking for nothing. I should be able to have them eating out of my hand, but I need info first. So, instead of emptying my guts, I say," You first."

Susan is surprised, but steps to the plate. "I am from Dallas, hence the accent, and I am a junior here. My family is in the oil business. I like Houston because it is near the beach." She has a sophisticated southern accent and holds herself in a courtly manner. She appears to know how to be with people of any station in life.

Megan is next. "I am Megan Plummer from Palestine Texas. My family grows roses. I needed to get out of that small town and enjoy the big city. I have an aunt and uncle here." She is a small-town girl with a *thick* east Texas accent that makes you think she is going to reach out and pinch your cheek like grandmas do. Wow!

Now, it is Carol Anne's turn, "I am Carol Ann Landry from Big Springs, TX or at least a ranch out there. I like my family's ranch but a change of scenery was needed. Houston just grows on you, and the shopping is fabulous here." She is self- assured and comfortable in her stylish dress, but probably she'd be comfortable in jeans and boots as well.

Okay, deep breath time. Here it goes. Oh wait, "Head up, shoulders back, look the problem straight in the eye, smile and believe that people want to be good." Thanks Mom.

"My name is Emerald Mist McCormick, aka Emmy, and I guess for now, I will tell you my home is near Washington DC. I am just eighteen, but I am not a true freshman since I have three hours from the Universidad de Salamanca, Spain, three hours from Loyola College, and twelve hours from John Hopkins University, Baltimore MD. My GPA is a 4.0 on a 4.0 system. I met Cindy at the dorms when we walked to tryouts for cheerleader, the Houston Honeys and Cougar Dolls together. We are both Houston Honeys, so we practice together, and then I go to cheerleading practice because I am the new Cougar mascot. I do have a car, but I rarely use it because I also have a driver on call. I don't know Houston well enough yet to not get lost. "

At the end of my speech, they sit up straighter and smiled big. I know I have them. They could tell I have enough money and the grades to fit into a sorority and survive. We exchange information, and Megan's explains I need to stop by the Pan-Hellenic office and register for open rush because regular rush was over. I tilt my head in inquisitive way and Megan continues with, Panhellenic is the organization that governs all the sororities and fraternities on campus. They also house records and can verify that you are a legacy and of course register you for rush. I nod in understanding.

I ask, "Is the office open now, and is it on the way to the athletic practice rooms?"

Carol Ann jumps right in and says, "Yes, it is and I can walk with you if you want."

I agreed and off we go.

Susan and Megan look a little angry at themselves for not thinking of that first, and Carol Ann is beaming.

Carol Ann and I make it to the office, and she introduces me to the president of Pan-hellenic, Candy Andre, who is a Phi Mu. Candy is a senior and from California. She looks part-Asian and part-something else, very exotic, but she has a Texas accent. I like her immediately, and ask, "Does everyone get a Texas accent when you live here?"

She smiles and answers, "Why yes, Is that a problem?"

I smile. I don't know if that is a good thing or not. I register and thank both girls, then excuse myself to practice. Being late is not good. I have a long afternoon and evening ahead of me.

I love practicing and rehearsing and getting it right. I am the only team member who lives at the Towers, even Cindy doesn't. She lives off campus and parks her car in the Moody Towers parking lot while on campus for class, then she moves it across campus for evening rehearsals. I ride with her to most practices.

My dorm, Moody Towers is at the very opposite side of campus from the gym. If I jogged back to the dorms, it is about fifteen to twenty minutes. This meant I have to cross campus in the dark or call a driver on the way home. I am not sure yet if I want these new friends to judge me, and a car pulling up with a driver getting out would defiantly turn a few heads. I decide to jog.

After my experience at John Hopkins, I am very cautious. I say a silent prayer that my personal angel, Archie is with me, and my thoughts of Eddie give me strength. Eddie is facing much worse. I think he is either on his way to Vietnam or already there. I pray each night for his safety as I seal my letter to him.

I am stay on the path, in the light, and will not stop. I am watching every movement around me. This is work. I like jogging but not on high alert like this. Every tree and bush is up for inspection. This is my second time to do this alone, so I feel a little more comfortable, but I am still nervous.

As I pass by the College of Education, which is half-way home, I notice it is darker here tonight. I wonder why? A large person steps out of the shadows in front of me. Shit! Should I scream? Should I run? He is smiling and coming to me. The pond in front of the admin building is to my right, and College of Education is now behind me. To my left there are the walkways to the UC, and on the other side of him are the oaks stand and my dorm. He is blocking my way. Time to make a stand. I just can't keep being scared. I have my keys in my hand, like Sean taught me, so I could use them as a weapon if I need to.

He reaches in his pocket.

Oh God is he pulling out a gun?

I am just about to attack when he says and waves, "Emerald, I am Clark. What are you doing out by yourself? Hey, stop. Are you going to give me a chance to show you my ID?"

I didn't wait. I am launching myself at him. I am not listening. He is putting me into a bear hug, standing very still saying very slowly as if I am a two-year-old he is trying to communicate with, "I am Clark Kent, and I have an ID that will tell you I am on your side. Please stop kicking me."

What? Did he say Clark Kent, like Superman, no way? Who in their right man would use that name unless it was real. I do, but he doesn't let me go. Not good. I take a deep breath and lean my head back to head butt him in the nose. I know a broken nose hurts. If he is Superman this will not hurt him or stop him. I guess he sees it coming because he shifts his weight and takes me sort of gently to the ground. By the time, I realize I am not hurt, and he is not hitting me, he has an ID in my face. Crap, this guy is a handler.

Clark says, "Okay they said your dad calls you his wild thing, I believe that now."

I look up at Clark and blink. Dang, all these handlers are cute. I know this sounds insane, but I have that moment of, "Oh gosh, he feels so nice laying on top of me, and he smells so nice. He is not Eddie, but this is the first man I have been this close to in the two years since Eddie left, and that manly presence is intoxicating."

That all disappeared when a woman's voice close by says, "Get a room."

Clark rolls off me, and we stand up .

FIFTY-TWO

LANGLEY OPS

- Clark and Mark have now made contact and will keep a watchful eye on Kitten mostly after dark when practice lets out.
- Sean thinks OPS is doing a good job.
- Tiger is settled in, and her security is working out well.
- Big Bird and Whitey still out of country.

FIFTY-THREE

Kidnapping in the Dorm

I TAKE A DEEP BREATH AND stick out my hand. "My name is Emmy. "Emerald" is just on paperwork. My mom chose the name because she is Irish and loves the mist that rolls off the bog in Ireland, so I am Emerald Mist."

Clark looks around and then looks me over as if he is checking me out to see if I am broken. He says, "With your dark auburn hair like your mom's, there is no mistake you are Irish and her daughter. Add to that, your wildcat reaction, and I can see your personality did not fall too far from that tree."

"Are you kidding me? You know my mom? Is she here? I look around for her or a car she could be in. My mom is amazing, I am not as perfect as she is, and besides, she is *always* in control."

As I finish my rapid-fire explosion of words, Clark gets this Cheshire cat grin all over his face and says, "You just proved my point completely."

I shut up and remain silent when Clark says he is walking me back to the dorms.

As we walk, he explains, "I am going to check on you, daily." He calls it a "wave off". When he spots me, he will wave, If I do not wave back, he will approach quickly."

I am supposed to start tomorrow, but when I saw you alone, it worried me. We have had some chatter lately about soft targets being a bigger risk."

I ask him, "Am I a soft target?"

Clark smiles real big and says, "Yes, in both meanings of the word."

I smile and blush as we walk on. This man is going to be a real challenge to keep at arm's length because I like him, and the idea of him closer. I guess it is important for Clark to blend in, and his boyish Superman look does the trick. I notice other girls looking at my escort. He is all man and even might have super powers, well, at least over the female sex.

The Towers are the new dorms there are two, and each is eighteen stories high. I am on the eleventh floor. There is a beautiful lobby, or commons area, and a cafeteria on the first floor as well as a gym and study area in the basement. The center section between the two towers is only two floors.

Clark is talking, but I am not really listening—I am daydreaming again. I tune back in when he says, "I want to come to your room. Will your roommate be there?"

I answer, "Hard to know with her. She has a boyfriend, and she stays with him most of the time."

Gosh, I hope my room is not a wreck. He will be a good test of how to handle a man in my room. It's not very big—there are two desks, two beds, two chairs, and two closets. That's it. Well, there is a first for everything. Try to listen and be calm. Don't let him know he is the first to be in your bedroom, *alone* with you. Oh heavens, my head is wandering back to him on top of me and the things I wanted to do to him and have done to me. Oh Eddie, why aren't you here? When will my hormones settle down? It is kind of nice that I almost live alone.

Clark surprises me when he says, "Yep, you were placed with her on purpose.

I stop short. "What?" I am listening, but this revelation really caught my attention.

He shrugs, trying to act like he didn't just let me in on a secret. "Her family is squeaky clean. Her Dad is a retired general. It just so happens Karly is enjoying her newfound freedom and is expressing it by shacking up with some low life. That won't last long. Daddy just found out, and I am sure he will put an end to that."

Yikes, had I just destroyed her social life? I hope not. I ask, "So

Clark, how did you know about her boyfriend?"

He looks at me funny, pauses, and then says, "You did not rat her out. We already knew."

I let out a breath I did not even know I was holding.

The ride to the eleventh floor is excruciatingly long with many stops letting people in and out, mostly off, I am silent, thank gawd, and so is Clark. One girl in the elevator looks him up and down like he is candy she wants. I feel possessive. He is nice looking in an old kinda of way. I would guess he is i his late twenties.

I am glad when she gets off the elevator. As she steps off, she looks back with a sigh and a wink. I did not want her to know what floor we are going to. Clark doesn't even seem to notice her.

As we approach my door, I know we will be alone. No lights under the door. Mmmm, I like this idea. Of course, I can't get the key to work, so I look like a nerd fighting with this small mechanical device, the keyhole. All of my girl parts are talking to me and I cannot seem to focus on getting the key in the dreaded keyhole.

Clark steps in close, puts his hand on mine, and says, "I got this."

Oh, how true this is just not in the way he means or is that *exactly* how he earns it? I turn to speak, he steps even closer — so close we are touching. I can feel his hot breath against me, and I can smell his delicious scent. I look up into his beautiful, brown eyes and wait. He takes a deep breath and pushes the door open.

I never saw it coming, and neither did Clark. The lights were off, but the drapes are open. I can barely see my roommate at her desk, something is very wrong. She is gagged and taped to the chair. Her eyes are like saucers, darting side-to-side. I try to push past Clark, so I can undo the tape and rescue Karly from the chair. But Clark puts his hand out and pushes me back. I land outside the room on my butt, and the door shuts in my face. As it closes, I see the two dark figures descend upon Clark. What is happening? Flight or fight. I think Karly is screaming now. Clark is inside and yells, "Run, Emmy, Run."

I am running away. Flight is my choice this time.

Each floor is the same in the dorms, a big square with rooms on the perimeter. This layout gives all the rooms a window. The showers, tubs, sinks, and toilets are in the middle. This is the girl's dorm, so as I pass the community bathrooms, two girls step out. They have all the necessary toiletries for an army in their shower caddies.

I hesitate and chance a look over my shoulder and see two men emerge from my room at the end of the hall. Oh no. As I fly by the two girls; they attempt to step out of my way and begin to verbally assault me. I want the toiletries to become weapons aimed at my pursuers, so I rip the plastic caddies away and throw them, hoping some might explode into a slippery mess in front of my potential attackers. It won't completely stop them, but it will slow them down. The indignant girls help without realizing. They are angry with me, but seeing these men on the floor after curfew changes their focus to the two men following me. I can hear them yelling and trying to detain, them so security officers will take them away. I hope they do.

I hit the stairs go down as fast as possible. I can run forever — I am strong and in shape, but the thought of eleven floors is still daunting. After six floors or so of running, I decide I need to take a minute to catch my breath. I know there are two stairwells in each tower, so I can exit this floor whatever it is, and run down the hall, then enter the other stairwell and continue on. As I pass the elevator, I push the button just in case it is there. No luck. I keep running. I open the door to the other stairwell, and just as I step in, I run smack into a man. A tall man, not just any tall man, but the one who rolled down the grassy hill with me at John Hopkins University. This time, I recognize him. Caesar.

He has a death grip on me. He says, *"La Tengo vienen rapidamente a la escalera transera del la parte. Estamos en el 5 to piso."*

Think Emmy think. *Tengo,* is to have, *rapidamente* means fast, *escalera* means stairs. Crap, Caesar is telling someone where we are, and that he has me. He has me so close, I can see the earpiece he is using to give orders.

He then smiles that familiar grin I fell for in Spain and says to me, *"Mi amor, mi amor hermoso."* Again, he is using his soft sensuous voice I remember so well. It is revolting this time.

Seconds later, the two men who were chasing me appear with giant, greasy smiles. Rapidly in Spanish Caesar says they need to leave now. We began moving. I am not going without a fight, but I will bide my time. Moments later, we step into the hallway of another floor and into a room. I can see out the window, and we are on the second or third floor. I began to scream, but he puts his hand on my mouth, pushes himself against me, and onto the bed.

If this had happened in Spain last summer, I would have been thrilled, but today, I am terrified. Who is he? Why is he here, doing this? My dad will kill him. Where is Clark? Is he ok? Oh God, Karly. Is she okay? Did his thugs hurt them?

I need to calm down and think. I need to make him relax, so he will release me, maybe enough to get away. enough to maybe get away.

FIFTY FOUR

Langley OPS

- Kitten is compromised.
- Clark sent out the alarm and it is a fluid situation.
- Karly is Ok and tells us Caesar is a part of this.
- Houston has a detail on its way.
- Mark and Sean are leading the team with Clark's help.
- Mark and Sean are two minutes from campus.
- More intel as we get it. We will be on head mics for this.

FIFTY-FIVE

Taken

CAESAR LOOKS DIRECTLY INTO MY eyes, smiles, and kisses me.

I let him. I even join in. I am hoping it will make him relax and take this down a notch. It does and it doesn't — he does relax for a moment until his henchmen react to the kiss.

Even though they are speaking Spanish, I know they are saying I like the kiss and so does he. I am pulled up and on my feet without me even realizing. He tells one of the guys to go check on our getaway car.

I am just about to scream again when Caesar says, "Don't scream, that will make me have to stop, you and that means drugs or a gag or hurting you. I really don't want any of those to happen."

He is right. I have to be smart and getting hurt or drugged will not help me. I don't think I can take him in a fight, and three of them make that a no-brainer.

I smile and ask, "Who are you really? Why me? Is Caesar your real name? I would have come willingly with you had you just asked."

His reply is shocking, "After John Hopkins, I figured you would not come near me."

I want him to trust me. I lie. "I really didn't know that was you at John Hopkins until just a few minutes ago."

He asks, "If you did not know, then why so much security?"

I look at him like he is crazy. A smile came across his face, he said, "You are an important *little* girl."

I yell at him, "I am not important!" I am pissed. No, I am hurt. He called me a little girl. Until then, I thought he thought of me as a peer and a woman not a little girl. I can't help myself when, I very firmly say, "You did not treat me like a little girl in Spain."

He turns slowly, smiling a slimy smile, just like the other men. Where has the Caesar I thought I knew, gone. Is this the real Caesar? Now, I am angry, and my connection to him is gone. I am not about to let him know that he had gotten to my heart and soul. I need to survive. I need to be important enough for him to not hurt or kill me. I realize he is waiting on me to answer him. He asks again, "If you are not so important, then why so much security? I think you are."

I have no truthful answer that will help matters, so I lie again, "My dad is worried about the racial unrest here in Houston, so he asked for me to have a constant minimal security check. Just to visually see I am okay. But, this craziness will change all that." I continue on, not letting him discount my explanation. "Okay I have answered your questions, Try answering mine. Who are you? I mean who do you work for?"

FIFTY-SIX

HOUSTON OPS

CLARK FUMBLES WITH HIS RADIO, announcing, "I am okay. Kitten is alive and still in the building." He pauses as he listens to the Houston OPS supervisor in his ear bud, answering their question. "I know where she is because I put the tracing device in her pocket when I took her to the ground." Another pause. "I will explain why I took her down when we get her back. I can tell by the signal that she is on the south side of the north tower. I just can't discern what floor. She has tracking device number fifty-two in her front pocket. As long as it is not found, we all can track her." Again, he listens. "Yes, Karly is fine. She is just scared and in shock. The EMTs have her, and she will be checked out at Ellington and then flown out from there."

Clark orders the other men where to search. She was mine to take care of, and I lost her. These guys spoke Spanish. So, they had to be from a Spanish-speaking country. Karly says Caesar is here, so they could also be from Spain. Emmy's parents have worked in all of those countries, except Spain. Emmy did run into Caesar in Spain, so I believe it is one and the same threat.

Clark's head is spinning not only from the situation but also from the confirmation with the suspects in girls' room. Is this about the Cuban submarine base or the election of the socialist presidential candidate, Salvadore Allende, in Chile. It really doesn't matter, they have her. There are many exits to cover. Each floor is being searched, so it's a matter of time. The front is being covered by a team, and there is no other way out. Oh wait, the basement in the gym has emergency exits plus the alarmed exits at the base of each stairwell. Emmy is a fighter, and smart too. I hope it serves her well tonight.

Giving orders into his radio, Clark states. "There are three unsecured exits. All are in the basement of north tower, one in gym and one in each stair well." Two different voices come back calmly stating that stairwell one and two are secure. Clark takes off for the gym followed by two other agents who have caught up with him. Again, the radio comes alive with a male voice saying, "The gym door is standing open."

Clark stops and looks at his tracker. Standing in front of the gym on the basement floor, he feels sick. "As you can see on the tracker; she is no longer in the tower." He shouts into the radio, "Kitten is on the move. The tracker is moving slowly. Looks like Kitten is on foot heading towards University Center. Head north west through the trees. Unknown number of threats with Kitten. There were two in the room plus Caesar so at least three maybe more. My weapon was compromised in the scuffle in the dorm room. Pete gave me his spare.

FIFTY-SEVEN

Escape?

I NEED TO ESCAPE. CAESAR AND his three slimy friends are too many for me to take on. If someone would just come by, that would be enough of a distraction. I hit the ground hard. Nope, I am pushed. Caesar has my face pushed into the ground. He is whispering to the others. One goes left, "Thing One". I can see him in my peripheral vision, and I hear another leave the other way — that's "Thing Two". All that is left is Fish Face, and he is smiling at me. Caesar scolds him to watch for agents and not to grin at me. What did they see?

A moment later, I hear two shots and two grunts kind of close. Caesar grabs me, and off we go running. I can see the University Center through the trees.

Yes! There are people there all the time. I pick up speed with him. He looks at me like he approves of my willingness to run. Fish Face can run really fast, and he breaks through the trees before us, heading for the black sedan at the curb. Oh crap, crap, crap. The University Center is on the other side of the road. Will they shoot me if I can get past Caesar and sprint for the UC? I gotta try.

As Fish Face gets to the car, I hear another gun shot. He is hit, but not dead, and manages to get in the car. This is my chance, I turn on the speed. Caesar is barely keeping up, and he has lost his grip on me. I am free, but not home free. I see the black sedan, and I am going to head straight for it, then at the last minute, turn.

Maybe I might escape, and whoever is shooting can take care

of Fish Face and Caesar. Just before I break into the open, I am grabbed around the middle and pulled into a stand of palmettos. Dang, that hurt. No, not again. Now, who? This time, there is no conversation. He just lays, there holding me down. Mmmmm, he smells like a real man. So nice. Okay, Emmy, what are you doing? Stop thinking like that. I scold myself. I am laying funny, so I try to roll over mostly for comfort. He lets me. I am on my back on the ground, and we are face-to-face. Wow!

He smiles, but returns to serious, and he whispers, "I have Kitten. Bob out."

He smiles again.

A second later, I see Caesar above Bob's head with a gun. My mouth opens, and my eyes are about to pop out of my head when Bob rolls fast to the right. Caesar shoots, just missing us. Then, another shot, and Caesar falls to the ground next to me. He is hurt, but not dead. Bob reaches out and removes the gun and says, "Threat is down but not neutralized. Where's the cavalry?" That calvary arrives with Clark in the lead. Caesar is hit, but it's not a kill shot.

Caesar is cuffed, and Bob says, "I got this one. I don't like the ones who think about shooting me, I want him. "

Clark looks me over and sort of pats me down. It is nice. He stops abruptly when he sees me smiling at him.

I say, "Don't let me keep you from your work. Please be thorough".

His face slightly reddens. I smile big even bigger on the inside.

FIFTY-EIGHT

Houston OPS

- Kitten is recovered. Bob and Pete have Caesar plus two others in custody.
- All perps will go to Ellington to be flown to LANGLEY for questioning.
- Kitten and Karly are also going to Ellington for the night.
- Karly's father will arrive 0800 Friday for pickup.
- Sean will arrive 0800 to take Kitten to secure hotel to plan what next.
- EMT checked both girls.
- No physical issues except a few scrapes and bruises.

FIFTY-NINE

Safe? Not So Much

AFTER THAT BRIEF MOMENT, EVERYTHING is like we are fast-forwarding through what is left of the night. I have had a really long day, and now, a long night. I want to go to bed and just sleep for twelve hours, or more. But a cozy bed is not on the agenda yet. As we ride along, I hear someone talking about my room, and how it is being swept thoroughly now. So, no more dorm room for me. I am content to sit and lay my head on Clark's shoulder as we drive away from campus.

When we stop, I awake to the late night, early morning sights of a military base, Air Force maybe. I think it looks deserted. I hear Clark talking about Caesar and the other bad guys are being directed to an airfield to go to Langley tonight. I still want to just lie down and sleep some more. Did that EMT give me something to make me sleep or am I just that tired. I follow directions and go with the flow. Because Clark had been with me when I was abducted, he could answer the questions about how it happened. My turn will come and, it did. I go over what happened after I took off running. I figure if I tell it all, I can sleep. Wrong because the first set of investigators got the info they needed, then the next set asked if I would mind going through my story again. I really want to shout no. I want to sleep, but it is a rhetorical question.

So, I begin again. By the third telling, Clark saves me and says, "Your room is ready."

I could have kissed him. No, I could have really kissed him.

Instead, I follow him towards the cars. There are four vans.

Karly is getting in one, and I am in another. There is a short drive, and out we go towards what looks like an old motel. Clark stops before he gets to the door, and I almost run him over, He opens the door to a room and motions to stay still. He came back and says, "All is clear." Yeah! a bed, its mine. The EMT hands me water and a pill, he says take this it will help you sleep. I am sure I don't need anything. But I comply. Bed. Soft sheets, Smells nice. Sleep. All mine.

I wake to find a guard sitting in a chair, obviously dozing off but close enough so that if any noise happens, he could be at my side in literally a second. This bed smells old like a grandma house. Was I so tired that I thought that this smelled nice? last night. Hmmmm, let me see. I move my hand to the side table and knock the empty plastic cup to the floor. Nothing happens. I check to see if I am still in the clothes I had on last night before I attempt to get up. I am, so I slowly slide to the other side of the bed. I gently push the covers aside and swing my feet over the side. On the bed next to me is Karly asleep. She wasn't there when I laid down. I turn and look over my shoulder to check on the guard. He is still dozing maybe even snoring so I stand and begin to take a step.

"Where are you going?" a deep voice, from somewhere across the room., called out.

It isn't one I recognize. From the sitting area, a tall, really dark, Latino-looking man appears. A man I have never seen before."To the bathroom," I answer without a thought.

I don't stop to chat. I go straight in the bathroom, closing and locking the door. My suspicious, over-active mind begins to work. Why didn't the guard wake up when I spoke? Why didn't the tall man address me or call me by name? Was I really on a military base last night? Had I been drugged? Had I been moved and didn't know? Was that the bed I laid down in just a few hours ago? Where did Karly come from? Where is Clark? He was with me when I closed my eyes. He said he would not leave me. Should I try to get out the window? What is this in my pocket? Huh, it looks like the tracker that she had in her backpack at Woodstock. Where did this come from? Maybe it belongs to the good guys. I can only hope but not depend on that.

SIXTY

Houston OPS

CLARK CRAWLS OUT OF THE dumpster coming is face-to-face with a tall, black, homeless dude. Thank God for small favors. He helps Clark out and helps him to a phone without a word. Clark calls into Houston OPS. Kitten and Karly have been both compromised again. Agent Jefferson and Michaels are here. Dead in a dumpster. Need a pickup now and a team for the dead agents. I am okay, but hurry.

Clark continues after a moment of listening, giving an address of where he is. Emmy knew the wounded prisoner. She said he was in Spain and is the same person who attacked her at John Hopkins. According to her, he proposed marriage to her in Spain, but she was extracted before she answered him. That was two years ago. What did he want then? Better question, what does he want now? This could be personal. How is this happening? Why is this happening again? All of these questions are running through Clark's mind as he listens to the OPS supervisor pepper him with questions too.

"My wallet is gone. I have a giant knot on my forehead. Get a detail here quick." As soon as help arrives, I will find Emmy..er, Kitten. Almost as an afterthought, Clark reminds OPS she might still have the tracker in her pocket. It has a limited range, but keep it monitored.

SIXTY-ONE

Taken Again

I KNEW I COULD MAKE IT out the window, but could Karly? I can't leave her again. I don't know her well, but she deserves better than to be deserted again. Okay, be fuzzy, go back, lie down, and listen. I walk back out and go straight to the bed without a word. The military-looking guard on the chair next to the bed does not move, and the man on the other side of the room is reading a magazine. As I sit down, Karly's eyes open. I let my hair cover my face and hands signaling her to be quiet.

She is silent.

I lie down and feign sleeping. What next? There is something wrong. I have to make this guy believe I am asleep. I begin to breathe steady and slow with a bit of a snore. Hopefully, he will ignore me.

Thirty long minutes pass. and an American-sounding man comes in and talks to the tall, dark, Latin man. Thank God, he is American because they speak in English. I promise myself right then and there I will learn Spanish. He says Caesar is fine and the bullet went straight through him, but the other three are believed dead. The Latin-looking man, who the American calls, "Jose" wants to be relieved for a break. The American man says, Okay. Could Karly and I take him? Then what?

Let me evaluate the two men, then I can form a plan. I need a weapon. As I look around, I notice the chair, the end table, and the lamp. Any will do if l can get to them in time. I can't see anything else without moving too much. How strong are these two? Mr. American is too far away to see; I would have to sit up. He sounds young-ish. So, he is probably strong. I will need something really heavy to hit him with. What about the other guy who is sleeping? I roll over and really study this silent man next to my bed.

Take it slow because you are supposed to be asleep. Be quiet for a minute or two, then slowly partly open your eyes and take him in.

He is too still. Oh gosh, I think he is dead. I gotta know. Do I see any movement? Hmmmm, I don't see any rise and fall of his chest. Focus. Do I see the hair on his upper lip move? Nope. He's gotta be dead. I move my arm under the covers and push slowly, but firmly, at his left arm. Oh crap, he falls to the floor taking the lamp with him. It is loud enough to wake the dead. The thundering crash brings Mr. American to the bed.

Mr. American needs to believe I am asleep. He comes so close to my face; I almost break cover and scream. When I don't move, he comes closer and waits so long, I am worried. But then, he stands up and begins to drag Mr. Dead Guy away.

I am so scared. I don't have a plan. While Mr. American has Mr. Dead Guy in his arms and his back to me, I roll over to see Karly's wide-eyed expression of surprise. I motion to Karly to follow me. She does and the two of us get up and head for Mr American. I quietly pick up the chair and Karly as if on cue, picks up the other lamp, and together we attack Mr. American. Yeah he went down like Mr. Dead Guy. Uh, did we just kill him? Nope, there is a pulse. Oh shit, now what? I still do not have a plan complete one anyway. Well, truth be told, I am really just winging it.

Karly must be feeling the same way because she verbalizes what I am thinking. "Now what? "

The door out of this room has a big unknown behind it. Who and what is behind Door Number One? Door Number Two is the bathroom and the window. I look at Karly, and I know it is up to me. Her bravery is over for now. I put the chair weapon under the doorknob to the unknown. We head to the bathroom together. I lock the bathroom door, and we open the window.

SIXTY-TWO

HOUSTON OPS

CLARK HAS BEEN RECOVERED ALIVE.
Intel from Emmy, through Clark, is Caesar is behind this.

The homeless man is Charlie, a veteran. He was in the alley, he helped Clark get to us. He has been questioned and rewarded for his service. There is a two-man team to help him to a better life solution.

Two possible locations were being vetted. One of them — the ranch — seems best because of its isolation. The other — warehouse — has promise too, but Texans are notoriously friendly and mistaken as nosey, so a warehouse might raise suspicions. The ranch has lots of land and ultimate privacy. We are hoping the tracker is still in Kitten's pocket, so keep monitoring it as you approach each location.

One hour later, Clark is with the "ranch" detail, on the way to investigate that location. Mark and Sean are on their way to the warehouse location. The ranch team is heading west on Interstate IH10, out of Houston past Katy, TX. They will take the Eagle Lake exit and turn south. Flat, and flat, and more flat terrain, with clumps of trees around the houses. Oh, and don't forget the rice flat fields. This is not the privacy Clark had expected. It doesn't exist in this area the element of surprise evaporated as Clark realized that the approach to the ranch house will not be so easy. We will be seen approaching. What a pain.

To Clark's surprise, the ranch has a stand of trees at the entrance and around the main house, with lots of cover along the way. A command post is established, and small teams are to approach from all sides. The command post gets word while the warehouse had helpful intel on this group, no one was there. The intel looks like there are five or six henchmen, and Caesar is one of the leaders. This intel worries Clark. Why has Caesar worked so long on Emmy as a target? Does Karly know him too?

Clark turns to the command leader and tells him of his knowledge —and suspicions — about Caesar. To command leader's credit he picks up the phone and relays this information to all members there at the ranch and and also to Houston OPS.

Clark is glad to be on this team, rather than the warehouse team. He is brought back to the conversation with a jolt as Rick, the commander, slaps him on the shoulder and says, "Hey Clark, you are right. This Caesar guy knows both girls. Looks like he is Mr. Smooth and moves in after he befriends them." Rick turns to the others and fills them in. Rick listens to someone talking in his head piece signals for everyone to move. Clark's pocket starts to beep. It is the tracker. Rick looks at him, silently questioning about the sudden noise. Clark pulls it out and says tell Houston OPS, "My tracker on Kitten is beeping. She is here or at least the tracker is." Clark looks at Rick and says, "I think need to move in now."

SIXTY-THREE

Must Escape

"Karly, this isn't going to be easy getting out the window, someone will be coming back to check on us soon. We have to get a move on it. I know Caesar will come as soon as he can."

Karly smiles and says, "Yes, he is my boyfriend."

"Boyfriend?" I ask. I try to hide my surprise at this statement. I am sure my mouth flew open. Karly didn't seem to notice my shock and surprise.

"Yes, we met in Barcelona, Spain. He is the love of my life. We have so much in common. We spent five days and nights together in Barcelona."

Karly's smile says that she is proud of this day and night adventure. She seems to be reliving it as she tells me. Karly continues talking in a dream like voice. "My dad was there on some business thing. I was so bored at the hotel, and there he was at the pool. He kind of bumped into me, and I fell into the pool, but he rescued me. Well sort of. He is just wonderful. I don't understand how he fits into this. I want to ask him just what this is all about."

I am stunned. Her boyfriend? Where did my moments with Caesar fit into this story? I guess young girls with influential dads are his thing. I am really pissed now, and I don't have time to explain it to Karly. I just smile with my face, but my heart is being assaulted. Focus men can be scum, and Caesar is proving that.

I put the toilet lid down and tell Karly to climb. She does. I can see she is visibly shaking. Hell, so am I. Then, to the top of toilet. While Karly is climbs, I am pushing on the window to get it open completely. It is one of those that pivot styles and it is just big enough to slide through. I have locked the bathroom door, but it won't hold long. Karly sticks her head out the window, and then she seems to just slide out the window like she is on a waterslide at Schlitterbahn, faster than I think humanly possible. I am afraid to call out, and she is so quiet. I am terrified is there someone out there.

I scramble up on the toilet and over to the window. I put my hands on the window frame and just as I put them down, two hands grab mine and pull me out. I start to scream when a huge hand covers my mouth. I am pulled tight up against someone. When I look up, there is a battered Clark staring straight into my eyes. He has his fingers to his lips, insisting I be silent. I did. I am so relieved.

I can see Karly ahead of me being taken away, and Clark has me by the hand, and we begin running from the house. Will this day ever end? After a couple minutes, I hear gun shots. A lot of gun shots. I drop to the ground, and just like that, Clark has scooped me up in his arms. Now Clark is sprinting away from the building.

Clark and I make it to what I am told is the command center. Karly is there too. We both call our parents.

My parents are still out of the country, so I talk to one of Sean's guys.

He says, "Your parents will be informed of what was going on, and Sean is still in Houston. They will be worried but relieved to hear you are back in good hands."

Mike says, "I will take you to a safe house and stay with you until further instructions. Karly's dad has a copter coming for her."

How cool is that? What a sweet ride. I lean over and quickly and quietly explain to Clark, "Karly thinks Caesar is her boyfriend."

He leans back and whispers, "I know".

I blurt out. "You know? How?"

Clark looks at me and smiles, saying, "Sometimes, the info all comes together, and we can connect the dots."

I feel sad for Karly because she really believes Caesar cares for her. Before we leave, I can hear her defending him. She is loud, and I think she is talking to her dad. Wow, that could be me. I feel sick inside, and sad.

I turn to Clark and ask, "Should I tell her about my encounter with him in Spain?"

He says, "She is very young, and she needs a little more time to realize she, like you, were his target."

I whip my head around and stare at him.

He draws back from me. "Hey, what's up? You kind of look like your Mom when she is pissed."

I try to steady my voice as I speak. "Really, and how do you describe me? I mean, am I very young too? Do you feel sorry for this poor little girl who can't tell real people from phony people?"

I am up and walking away. I don't know where I am going, but I feel like screaming. Yeah, I know, Caesar is a good con artist, and I did fall for his story — he knows how to make a girl feel special. I'll give him that. I just didn't want to face the fact that he did it all the time. I mean, I knew him for months, not five days like Karly, I missed the subversive side of his life. How did I miss it?

So, I am really pissed with Caesar, and now, Clark too, for making me face my sheltered life shortcomings. I feel like the people watching a horror movie where the main characters head for the dark, cold basement, and you know that's where the bad guys are, but they don't know and go anyways. You want to know why they are going there. It seems so obvious now.

Clark catches up with me, he steps in front of me. I stop. He starts to apologize when I {turn both hands on his chest and just push. He wasn't expecting me to push him, he staggers back. I start to walk again. He starts to push me back, then thinks better of it. I stop and look at his hands and he drops them to his side.

"Look, I get it. I am just a part of your job, and an apology is not necessary. You save me. I am the dumb one here who should just be grateful you are here for me." I spit out. It stings to say this out loud but there you have it.

He takes my hand and leads me to a small room used for interviews, "Sit".

I do. I am really exhausted, so the small quiet room is a sudden relief I didn't know I needed.

He sits down knee-to-knee, takes both of my hands, and looks me in the eyes. "Yes, you are my job, and I do get paid, but you need to know I like your family and should have been reassigned in the rotation months ago, but I asked to stay on your dad's detail."

I just stare at him. By the look on his face, he needs me to say something, but I had no words for him. My head is filled with stupid questions and obvious answers, but the job thing has just never been said out loud, and it is weird to be treated as a person, not a child.

So, after a long pause, I say, "I just don't know what to say, maybe thank you, but that's not enough. You saved me."

He looked at me with that sad puppy dog look that makes you want to keep the stray puppy you might find, then, he says, "It's what your mom and dad say, and it works. It is nice to be able to level with you and tell you straight what's going on. You deserve to know. When you and Karly came out that window, you made our jobs so easy. Karly says it was your idea. That is so brave, and so like your parents."

I just smile, and he leans over and puts his hand on my cheek. It was nice.

I don't think it is awkward, but he moves quickly as if he thinks it is. He begins chattering about needing sleep and getting me out of this area, to safer territory. As we leave the interrogation room, Karly is being escorted to her copter ride.

She stops. She looks like she has been crying, and she hugs me. "Thank you, I can't wait to tell Dad all about you. You know, we can't share boyfriends. It just doesn't work."

I am more than startled.

My silence makes Karly look at me like I am a small child and tells me, "I hope you are ready to let him go because he is mine."

I guess I take too long to answer because she leans in close and whispers, "Understand?"

I just smile and nod. "He is all yours." She smiles in triumph.

SIXTY-FOUR

Houston OPS

- Karly is now on a short copter ride to a plane, going to her home state of North Dakota to meet up with family.
- Kitten in being moved to the Hyatt Downtown Houston with a secure team.
- Plans for her new residence are almost complete.
- Agent Kline, Day, and Wells have been added to the detail. They are to implement the trap.
- More intel on trap in briefing tomorrow.

SIXTY-FIVE

The Delicious Trap

———

WHEN WE ARRIVE, SEAN IS in the suite at the Hyatt. I smile and run to give him a big hug.

He holds me at arm's length and says, "You're not hurt?"

I look at the floor feeling embarrassed that I have caused so many people to have to rescue me, and say "Nope, if you don't count my feelings".

He pulls me in for a big brother hug. I cling to him, and I realize how long he has been there for me and how lucky I am. Clark gives Sean an update while I stand there and listen.

Then, as if they have choreographed it. They turn their heads in unison and say, "Go to bed. Tomorrow is a big day."

I obey. I don't have to be told twice.

I stop half-way to the bedroom, turn, and say, "Big day, what was yesterday? Nursery school? Let's see, I was grabbed, dragged, pushed down, and drugged, not to mention kidnapped not once, but twice."

They smile and point to the bedroom.

I go willingly. I soon realize I will have to tell my story again, and again, and again. Plus, I will have to identify all the bad guys. Some with photos, and some in a line-up. My room has a bag with some of my clothes in it; yeah someone has packed for me. No privacy in my world. I shower and fall into bed.

As I emerge the next morning from my room I stop and put my hands on my hips, and declare, "Okay, I will tell you two everything I know, but I have some questions that have to be answered first. I mean, now!"

"Can we eat breakfast first?" Sean whispers.

"Does this joint have room service? I can eat and talk." Clark moves to the phone and picks up a menu. "So what do you like for breakfast, Emmy?

Sean answers for me, "Order her orange juice, two eggs over-easy, two pieces of bacon, hash browns, and wheat toast with Strawberry jelly."

I stare at Sean, and so does Clark.

"What?" Sean is looking back and forth between us, "Unless Emmy has totally changed in the last month, that is what she likes for breakfast."

Clark laughs and then looks at me, "So, is he right?"

I nod. Note to self: Don't be so predictable.

"Okay, guys, here goes. What does my dad do?"

In unison they answer, "Classified"

"How about my mom?"

"Classified"

"Where are they?"

"Classified"

"Well, that's just great ! I am so informed. Hmmm, is the sky blue?"

They look at each other and say, together, "Yes, but not today. It is overcast".

So much for being treated as an adult. They are saved from a slow death of torture by room service. I stomp to the door. Clark arrives before me and waves me off. I bat his hand away, disgusted.

"What? Is the big bad wolf on the other side?"

Clark sighs, "Well if you must know Caesar is still at large."

I back up immediately. I could say was "Oh!"

It is just the guy with breakfast. He is a little taken aback with all the attention the tray got. He is yanked inside with his trolley and is questioned thoroughly. The trolley got the same treat mental thorough inspection.

When can I go back to the dorms? And class? And practice? And sorority meetings? Well and just my life?

Clark chirps in, "If you hadn't noticed it is the Friday before Thanksgiving week so no classes next week."

I hadn't thought about that. My time clock is just out of whack.

"Oh crap, I have to cheer at the football game this coming Friday. That is in a week. The University of Houston plays Texas A and M in Dallas the day after Thanksgiving. And I have to be at practice even without classes and trip prep on Wednesday." I start to spew out all kinds of commitments and classwork that are due soon.

Sean looks up and says, "We are working on that. It should be okay, but the dorms are out, so you will need a new nest." I am confused, my brain is just not getting it. I ask, "Huh, A new nest?"

Clark came over, sat down next to me, and says, "We are working on a new, safe place for you to live. It should be ready in a day or two."

As we sit quietly eating breakfast, my list of questions grows and grows. "Okay guys, Caesar is still a problem. That is very evident when Clark made it to the door first. I want a life. I am not going to change schools, so that new place better be right here in Houston. When I chose U of H, I had already been through a whole list of college ideas. I don't want to start again. I mean I couldn't go to the University of Maryland or John Hopkins or Loyola College or the Catholic University because of the closeness to Washington DC. Some of them were not my cup of tea anyway. No colleges in the capital cities. East coast colleges were on a case by case inspection. The idea of starting over is daunting, and I just don't want to do that again. Besides, I like Houston. There's a beach close, the city has lots to do here, and people are friendly in Texas. Mostly, I have made a life here and friends." No one answers my rant.

I snap my fingers in front of Sean's face and say, "Earth to Sean. Are you guys even listening?"

Clark smiles at my boldness with Sean, I continue, "Wow I've been talking but you have not been listening to me. It's time to plan, I want to be treated differently, so let's see if that can work. I am all ears."

Sean and Clark look back and forth at each other and get this goofy smile on their faces.

Sean looks and me, and says, "Okay"

Can this be true? Finally, someone thinks I have a brain. I get to help plan my life not be just told what to do.

"Your mom and dad think you should help," Clark adds.

Sean asks, "The question is can you do this." Sean seems to be looking inside my head. He has his serious look on. I have seen it many times when he is talking to dad.

I want to reach out and grab his collar to answer. He needs a good wake up call. Instead, I use extreme control of voice and body.

"Yes I can do this. Where do we start?"

Sean leans back in his chair, takes a big breath, but I interrupt. "What about Lucy."

Sean looks at me crossed-eyed, "What about Lucy? Did Caesar mention her? Do you know something we don't?"

I guess my expression told all. "Uhhh, I just wanted to know if she has had as many situations as I have?"

Clark smiles as he begins talking about Tiger aka Lucy, "Your sister is in a public school. She lasted about a week at your old high school. She said the nuns kept saying, "Emmy this," and "Emmy that," and she wanted to go to high school without your shadow hovering over her."

I interrupt, "Is she safe in a big, public high school?"

Sean put his hand on mine and says, "Let him finish. We have done this before; we have her covered."

I realize, I am being a little kid with all my emotions attached.

I turn my head towards Clark. and nod, and say, "Okay go on"

I sit back and try to relax. Pushing my breakfast plate away, because eating anymore breakfast is out of the question."Let's try this again. At her new high school, there are two retired navy seals, and they have agreed to be our daily eyes and ears until this Caesar thing is solved. As far as we can tell, she has not been approached. Besides, your sister is on the rifle team and is armed at least some of the time. Oh, by the way, she the most accurate shot on the team, much to the disappointment of the rest of the team. That's probably because she is the only girl. Her new boyfriend is the second-best shot, and his best friend is third best, and both boys have black belts. The trio travel to and from school together. Her boyfriend is strong, very protective, and attractive. He is also the leader of their little group, but he is not the brightest bulb in the group. Thank goodness, his best friend is and he listens to his friend. "

My mouth is hanging open, so I close it, "Does she know you know all this?"

"We don't think so. She is really happy in her world and doesn't seem to be as adventuresome as you. Uhh, not that adventuresome is bad. She just seems content with a quieter lifestyle. You are outgoing and never meet a stranger like you mom. You and your mom are strong will women."

He called me a woman. I am excited and sort of proud that I am labeled a woman and not a little girl. Yeah me! Lucy's relationship with your mom is more atypical of a rebellious teen than your adult like relationship you have with your Mom. She adores your dad like you, but your Mom is another thing altogether. She tends to fight rather than talk to her about everything. Boy, she has a temper I probably have said too much."

I am speechless. My head is trying to take all this in. I am just staring at both of them,

Clark wakes me from my silent reflection by patting my hand.

Before he can speak I say, "Okay I can see you plan and know a lot about us but why? I mean what do my parents do, know, or have that makes it so important to stop them through me. Please don't say "Classified."

Sean chirps in first, "Most of the real hard facts are classified, but let's talk about what you already know. Tell us what you know or *think* you know"

Hmmm, that makes sense, I am silent, maybe a little too long for them, as I process recent events and information.

Sean clears his throat.

I am ready for this planning meeting to move forward; I feel relieved to begin.

"Okay I know my parents are out of the country a lot - South

America, Cuba, Puerto Rico, sometimes Europe. They are very interested in where the Nazis are. I thought they were captured after WWII, but maybe not. They keep an eye on what is going on in Vietnam, but I don't think they go there. Caesar speaks Spanish, I'm not sure he is really from Spain. However, that's where I met him. My parents know a lot of important people in Washington, DC, and they speak foreign languages. Dad speaks Spanish and German. I think mom speaks just Spanish, but she fakes not knowing too much. Not too long ago, they were both injured, and that really worries me. I am sure there is more, but I can't think of anything else right now."

Sean and Clark are looking at me with surprise on their faces. "That will do for now, your observations are correct so let's work from there. Okay?"

Sean waits for an answer.

I throw my hands in the air and say, "Do I have a choice?"

"Not really, Caesar is still out there, and, for some reason, he is fixated on you. Sure, he wants the leverage he would 'have' over your parents if he could capture you, but we think it's you, or at least you as a conquest *personally* is motivating him right now. That need to "have" you makes him vulnerable but dangerous."

This is dangerous for me and I am sure it shows on my face. "So, I am the bait whether I like it or not."

"Well, yes." Clark answers quietly sensing my 'deer in the headlights look'

I know I am missing something; I sit there for a moment playing with the cross around my neck, finally I say, "That kind of scares me. What I don't get is what does he want from *me*. I get my parents know stuff he wants, but what do I have? I don't know what I may know."

Both men slowly turn and look at each other, and then, back at me like a have just grown two heads.

"What?" It was so weird how both looked at me, with the same smirk, and devilish, sleazy predators look on their faces. It took me a minute, I blushed and say, "Ohhh, That."

Clark is the first to answer, "Yeah that, do you need more information? So, we're going to give you to him, uh with your permission"

I can't believe my ears. I can't believe they think I am going to say yes to being his sex toy.

"You what? You're going to give me to him? Did my dad approve this? And mom?"

Sean smiles, "Well yes, that's the simplified plan."

I didn't smile back. I could feel my face heating up. I am about to explode. I want to be treated as an adult but an exploited women.

Clark cut Sean off from saying more, or me exploding, by saying, "Well, not really give you over for real but he will think so. We think his ego will believe you are there for the taking, and we have gone home thinking you are safe, thinking he has been chased away."

I am squirming inside, and I hope my fear and anxiety are not showing too much.

"Okay I'm listening how do you give me to him, but not really?" I can't believe my ears. Are these men crazy?

Clark continues, "Here's the plan. You have an apartment now, not a dorm. So, it will feel easier to get you alone. You will go to school and your activities, but we will track you. And your live-in boyfriend will be in all your classes, so he will be with you all the time."

An apartment all to myself, sounds nice. Sometimes, the dorms are so noisy, and the communal bathroom is not my cup of tea. I always feel like I need to clean before I use the shower or sink. I am smiling as all this is running through my head when I finally land on the words "live-in boyfriend."

I jump up, put both hands out, and sort of shout, "Whoa, wait, what? My dad has approved a live-in boyfriend. What planet do you guys live on? I can't believe that flies with him."

Sean takes my arm. "Sit down. That plane already left the airport. He has approved this plan, yes, even your mom is onboard."

I could say I am stunned, but that would not even touch how I feel. I decide to push all their buttons. "So, which one of you got this detail?" That moment was just funny. The look on both of their faces is amazing as they both just stare at me.

There is a knock at the door that broke the classic moment of shock. I snicker. I have shocked them both. Hurray for me. That victory is short-lived when not one, but three fabulous men are let in the hotel door. They all look around my age. Number One is a blonde surfer dude with all the muscles that go with surfer dudes. Number Two is tall, dark, and dreamy. His eyes are the kind you fall into and never come out of. Number Three is taller than I am. He is about six-foot-something and looks a little like Caesar, but much more perfect in every way. I am staring. They all smile at me.

Sean stops me enjoying the eye candy by saying. "So Kitten, who gets the job?"

I just look at him. Clark butted in and says, "She gets to talk to each one alone, if she wants before she chooses."

I just keep looking from one man to the next in disbelief.

Sean smirks. "You wanted to get involved, so here you are, involved.

Trying to hide my embarrassed shyness and utter disbelief, I calmly state, "Let me get this straight. I have to pick one of these men to be my live-in boyfriend, so jealous Caesar will intrude and try to snatch me again."

Mr. Dreamy Eyes says, "Try, but not actually take you. One of us will be there, and I mean *right* there, with you all the time."

Wow, no double wow, I pick one to live with in an apartment by ourselves until Caesar makes his move. In the meantime, I go to school and go on co-habiting until it happens. I look up to see five sets of eyes staring down at me.

"Hmmmm, okay, let's get this show on the road. Who's first?"

I get up and go to the bedroom to do the, um, interviews.

Mr. Dreamy Eyes follows me into the bedroom. I hear him say to the others, "May the best man win."

I sit on the end of the bed. He closes the door, and I swallow hard.

He is just checking me out. Then, he steps up, stands inches from me, and takes my hands.

He smiles, "My name is Charlie Wells, and I don't bite, unless you want me to. I think you are brave to do this. I am not sure, I would like it if my sister had to do this. I know to be convincing; we will have to be intimate, but I will only go as far as you want well, only as far as well, we'll play it by ear. This assignment is something I have never done before either, so I would like to try something that might help."

My brain is screaming stop, "intimate" like how intimate? I try to smile, I asked for this, to be part of the planning. Can I really do this? I can!

I blink and look up into those dreamy eyes. This is like shopping for a new puppy. I think all three are adorable. Maybe, I can have all three. FOCUS. This is a job, but a nice one for me.

Charlie interrupts my thoughts, "You see the three of us talked and think you need to trust us and be attracted to us to make it believable to Caesar. You know, to make him jealous and want you right then and there."

Okay, I can see that. But, how does he plan to do that? I look up, and find he is just waiting on me to talk.

"I can see that logic. What is the plan?"

He steps closer, lifts my chin, and kisses me.

I melt into him. I could feel him relax and deepen the kiss. Time stood still. I really don't know how long we kissed but it was nice.

He steps back, smiles and says, "I hope I get more kisses."

Before I could answer, he is gone. Surfer dude aka Sterling Kline is next. He says the same thing about the kiss test and steps close.

He can kiss, too. He pulls me in closer and whispers, "So nice." Before he turns to leave, he whispers again, "Pick me!"

Caesar's twin came last, and he too explains in his deep Texas accent about the kiss test. His beautiful Texas accent is so enticing, I am all in listening to him. Marty Day says, "The kiss is my idea. And, little Lady, Sean and Clark do not know about the kiss test. Let's try to keep it our little secret. I'd hate to get skinned alive by them two. We think the girls we date should make that final decision of which someone to date by whose kiss they enjoyed most.

Caesar's twin steps close and speaks in Spanish to me, " You are beautiful my love— *Eres Hermoso mi amor.*"

I stiffen.

He steps back, "I have frightened you, I am sorry. I am told I look a lot like this Caesar fellow, and you will either react really good or really bad to me. I can feel I'm not the one, right?"

I look up with a sad smile, lean in and kiss him then step back. "You are right. You do remind me of Caesar, but it's not your look. It's what you said. What you said is what *he* said to me before *he* kissed me. It reminded me how much I dislike him for playing with me."

Marty leans in and we kiss again.

He steps back, "Mmmmmmm, that was nice. Happy me, I got two kisses. One given and one taken. Whoever you pick is a lucky man."

My heart is beating at break-neck speeds. Choose? Wow, surfer dude is cute, but kissing him would feel too much like kissing Tootsie's brother, Bob. Marty had me thinking of Caesar too much, not a safe thought. I guess it is Charlie then. Those dreamy eyes are so nice, and he just feels right. I like he has a sister to make him maybe have a moral conscience. Stupid thought. Remember, this is a job for him. Its work not play. Get over it.

When the door closed behind Marty, all I could think of was which one? Now reality sets in. Eddie's smile fills my heart and soul. Will he understand? Should I tell him? He doesn't say much about his social life. He has to have one, right? I have to trust that Eddie will see the need for this plan. Can I write him? what happened if someone got that letter that shouldn't? That could cause all kinds of problems.

Twenty minutes later, the six of us make plans.

Sean leads the discussion, "The apartment is one of those four-plexes by Rice University. Charlie, you and Emmy will live upstairs in Unit Four. Marty will be below you in Unit Three, and Sterling will be across the alley in Unit One. The owner lives in Unit Two and is retired Navy. The parking lot holds six cars. Each unit has an outdoor porch in back. The back door is the safest entry, but it is also the most hidden too."

Oh my God, this is really happening! I am not married well, not yet, and I am living with a man. How am I going to explain this to Eddie? I have to think about that. I shouldn't be so excited, but I am.

SIXTY-SIX

Houston OPS

- Sean and Clark have chosen Charlie Wells to be in the apartment with Kitten.
- Agent Day and Agent Kline will be in charge of surveillance in the other two apartments.
- Check to see when you are assigned as relief.
- Agent Wells is enrolled is the same classes as Kitten and will be with her twenty-four seven
- Intel reviled that Caesar entered the country through Mexico at Acuna crossing.
- All borders have him on their arrest on sight list.
- Big Bird and Whitey are concerned.
- Keep a tight perimeter around Kitten.

SIXTY-SEVEN

The Apartment

———◆———

THE APARTMENT IS CUTE. IT is a shot-gun floor plan. You come in the front door and go up a flight of stairs that has one turn back. The landing has a place for a small bench and a place for umbrellas. Just inside the door is a small living area with a sofa, and a chair, and a TV. It is so cozy. Charlie and I just drop our bags. He checks the whole place out, closets and all, I guess for intruders. Then he runs back out for the rest of our luggage.

The next room is the kitchen—it is small but it works. Then the bathroom is painted in soft butter yellow. And finally, the bedroom decorated in shades of blues from denim to pale blue. There are windows in each room because we look out over the alley between the other two apartments. As I look out a window, I see Charlie with the other two bags, and Marty has stopped to talk to him. As my gaze raises, I see this older man directly across the alley staring at me. I smile, but he closes the curtains. That is odd. He doesn't seem too friendly.

Charlie is just coming in the door when I get back to the living room. He is closing the blinds and shutting the drapes. He turns and smiles. That makes it kind of dark in here, there is a lump in my throat. He smiles again before moving through the kitchen and into the bedroom with his luggage. He turns, motioning for me to follow.

I swallow hard, pick up my luggage, and follow. The two windows in the kitchen have the drapes open and blinds up, so there is a blast of light as I pass through. "Why didn't you draw those too?"

Charlie sits of the edge of the bed, watching me notice the blinds open in the kitchen, "Caesar has to see somethings but not all."

Oh, that lump is back again. Charlie pats the bed where he is sitting. "I will take the side of the bed that is closest to the door for safety."

BED!!!! We are sleeping in the same bed. I look up at him and he can read my face.

He stands, and comes closer, and whispers, "I am *sleeping* here, nothing else. You are safe." He kisses me on the top of my head takes my hand and walks me into the kitchen. He points at the clock, then points to his ear. Then, he leads me to the living room and shows me another bug. He leans in real close, whispering in my ear, "Kisses are too quiet to be picked up that makes me happy because your kisses are ohh sooo nice."

I melt as he kisses me and he says, "I like this practice time thank you."

Here I go again sleeping with a man and not getting all the benefits. Charlie is so considerate. He has a way of staying out of my space, so I can dress and not feel like he is ever-present. But, as the nights go by, Charlie notices, I am not sleeping very well. He so sweet.

That third night, he rolls over an says, "Emmy, roll over and face me."

I do. I gulp. The drapes are allowing a small beam from the outside security lights, casting a heavenly glow across his face. It was an angelic look until our eyes meet.

His eyes tell the story. "I can't do this without sleeping closer to you, but my job says I shouldn't. So, let's talk about it." I move closer, and he rests his hand on my hip.

I guess I moaned because he takes that acknowledgement as a 'yes' and move closer. We kiss for a minute, I turn over, and he snuggles up close. I close my eyes, he kisses my neck, and I fall sleep.

The next morning, I am rested. I have slept, and Charlie is in the kitchen. He is whistling as he cooks. The eggs and bacon smells great. Without a thought of the drapes being open, I walk out in my short nightshirt that just barely covers all my girl parts. I come up behind Charlie, leaning around him to look at the skillet of delicious smelling food. He whips around, steps between me and the window and holds me.

He leans over, whispering in my ear, "We have company."

I stiffen.

"No worries, Kitten. The guys are on it. Stay cool. Make us look real."

What does real look like? I have seen sexy moves in the movies, so why not try one? No harm, right? I can play at this. Since his back is to the window, I put my hands under his T-shirt, lowering them to hold onto his cute butt.

He stiffens, and I mean stiffens. Then, he picks me up and carries me to the bedroom, kissing my neck as he walks.

Damn. Thank you for the invitation, and you can do that any ole time because I really like it a lot. Right now, I want you but you need to get dressed in case things cause us to have to move from here."

I dress and smile inside because I like the power I just experienced with Charlie.

Whoever had been on the roof slipped away before Marty or Sterling could get there. Retired Navy Landlord is as surprised as we are that someone was on his roof. The access doors to the roof were locked and did not show any use.

My boys, I love calling them that, decide he gained access from the adjoining roof. It is a good sign that our plan is working. I am not so happy, but I know it is just me worrying no, I am just scared—terrified, actually.

I insist Charlie recheck all the doors and windows.

He comes to the sofa, "You're scared, aren't you?"

I nod.

He moves closer and pulls me into him. "I am here. You are safe."

I sit there in his safe arms, for how long, I am not sure. The sweet silence is broken by a knock at the door. Charlie jumps up and goes to the door.

"Delivery for Miss McCormick," came a voice from outside.

Charlie opens the door to Marty.

I gasp, jump up, and run.

Both stand there looking at me run. Charlie runs after me.

I blush and start sputtering apologies before they even realize why I have jumped and ran. Charlie grabs me, pulls me close. Then, puts both hands on my face and looks me straight in the eyes, close. Marty came in close too.

Charlie whispers, "You are shaking. What is it?"

I turned my head and just stare at Marty.

Marty smiles a hurt sad smile and says in his deep East Texas draw, "Kitten, it will be okay, and I am no danger to you."

Charlie still doesn't get what is wrong.

I step towards Marty and hold his hands.

I look in Marty's sad eyes, "You are so close to his look for a moment I thought you were him. I am so sorry." Charlie just looks at me, then to Marty. "Oh, I get it."

Marty's delivery is a small box. Marty explains, "In the commotion earlier I forgot to give Emmy this, it's from your parents."

Mom sent a necklace. I read the note out loud. "This has been blessed by the pope. This angel standing in front of a cross, it is to keep you safe. I know you have many angels guarding you but this angel is from your dad and I. We are guarding you too. Please, wear it every day, so we will be with you always. Also, please hug your angels for me."

I look up at the boys with tear filled eyes.

Dad's part of the note says, "The young men guarding you are the best of the best. I look forward to shaking their hands and thanking them for all their work and dedication. Listen to them, they know what to do to keep you safe. Wear your Angel everywhere."

My mom wears jewelry, but not a lot, so I wondered what caused her to buy a piece for me Charlie and Marty look at it closely, and nod in approval.

I really miss them. They are in Rome, and bound for Spain, France, then Germany, but they will be home for Christmas. I will see them then. My heart needs that.

When I look up, I realize Charlie and Marty were waiting on me.

"What?" I ask.

Charlie blinks, then moves closer. "Two things, first, this Angel is more than you think."

"Yes, Mom wants me to wear it, I will. for her to ask is an important request, add to the request that my dad wants it too, I will honor their request and wear it always."

Charlie smiles and try's again but more direct, "This angel is different."

"I know. It is blessed by the Pope."

Charlie puts his hand over the necklace in my hand and flips it over and points at a small raised area on the back. "Emmy, this is a tracker. It is very new and powerful. Karly's tracker saved you two once, so your mom and dad felt like you should have one too. Here it is in an easy way to have it on you always."

Wow, Do I feel slow. Again, my parents are so careful with me, I love them.

Marty comes over, sitting close. "You and I need a safe word, so even in the dark, you will know it's me, not Caesar. Charlie thinks it should be just one word. I think it should be a question you ask, and I answer it with a set answer. Or, a question I ask, and you answer one way for you are okay, and another if you are not. What do you think?"

My mind went a million directions. All I could say is, "Okay."

Charlie asks, "Okay? What, or which?" Charlie throws his hands up and just sits on the sofa pulling me along. "That was not a yes, or no, kind of answer. You have to tell us who you agree with."

I look at both men. "All I think it will be helpful if I have them all."

Charlie looks at me crazy-like. "All? All what?"

This time it is my turn to show them the plan. "Marty, you should have a one-word close-up code and the other two ideas should or could be used by all three of you. You, Marty, Charlie and Sterling. What do you think.?"

Both are still staring at this new, take-charge Emmy. "How

about, Marty, if your safe word would be something that really makes use of your East Texas draw. Which is something Caesar will not think of."

Marty looks at me with a sideways smile that could have been on Caesar's face too. Then, he leans in and breathes in my ear, "You are finger-licken good."

I pull back, and blush, he grins a big smile, then roars in laughter. I hit him, and Charlie just stares back and forth at us.

"I love it; it will be our little sexy secret." I wink at him.

He roars in laughter again.

"I may not get to be here with you, but that is second best. Can we practice?" Marty asks.

I hit him again, and he roars again. He has the best sounding laughter, it's so contagious.

The phone rang, and Charlie picks it up. "Yes, you can. Thanks."

Seconds later, Sterling arrives and wants to see Marty practice. I stare. He grins and points to the bug in the living room. I groan. Not a private moment here.

We brainstorm for the other two safe sentences and come up with an I'm okay answer and an I'm not okay answer. It is so silly that it is perfect.

It went like this, "Hey did you watch that Sesame Street episode with Big Bird in it yesterday?

"Yes, I did" meant I am okay, and "No, I didn't" meant come now, but be cautious, and "I don't know what you are talking about." Meant get your ass here now." This made perfect sense, not only to me but to all three men. They thought so too because "Big Bird" is my mom's call name.

The identifying sentence took longer to compose. We finally got it. We needed a one-sentence question and one-sentence answer. This allowed me the ability to change up the answer to get help without alerting anyone else. It should go like this if all is well, "Emmy your Dad is concerned you are going to *all* your classes, and not just the ones you like."

I should answer, "Well, I've been late a couple of times, but I am going to *all* of them." If I deviated, even a little, someone would be at my side as soon as possible. I hope I will never have to use any of these safe words or sentences.

I took a deep breath and let my breath out. "I hate to bring up delicate subjects, but I need to ask some questions."

All three heads swivel to look at me. "What? what's that look about? I just think we need a plan for the next game and my classes.

They all exhale at the same time.

"Really? What was that about? You three make me nervous. Why were you holding your breath? What's up? What am I missing?"

Sterling was the first to speak. "We think Caesar is on a timeline, and it's catching up with us, well, I mean you."

"So you think he is going to make a move on me soon? Or was that man on the roof was the beginning? Do I look freaked out, because I am."

They all look at each other, and then Charlie takes a turn, "I'm here day and night just for that reason."

"I get it — you guys are keeping me safe. I also know I am your job. But, just why am I so interesting to these guys?"

Again, they all exchange crazy, confusing looks.

"What? I am so tired of this. What? Why? What would make my parents approve of one of you three *guys* living with me? I just don't get it. Come on, at least try to explain some of it. Give me *something*."

At once, all three men exhale. I am so done with this. I get up and stomp off to the bedroom. I just want to scream. Instead, I just throw my pillow against the wall. My stuffed teddy bear goes next. When the bear hits the wall, there is a loud cracking noise, and two small batteries fall out. I am surprised my soft bear has batteries because it doesn't have any reason to. I pick it up and explode back into the living room with a roar. I am holding the bear by its arm with a wire sticking out of it in one hand and two batteries in other. "

You pervs. Just what is the meaning of this?"

All three stand at once and put their finger to their lips in the shhh mode, coming up to me.

Charlie speaks first. "I'm not a perv, but these other two could be. All I want is you alone in the bedroom."

My eyes pop out of my head, and I open my mouth to speak, but nothing comes out. What the hell? Yeah right, in your dreams. All these answers run through my head.

Charlie kisses me, then pulls away, puts his hand gently over my mouth, shakes his head. The kiss is amazing, and I melt into him. He knows I am affected by the kiss. He looks into my eyes and holds me closer. feel his heartbeat race. Did the kiss do anything to him or am I just a job. Was that kiss for my nerves or his?

He looks over my shoulder, "Social hour is over guys, Emmy and I need some quiet time."

Marty and Sterling start for the door, saying their goodbyes, plus a few sexual jabs about needing alone time. The door opens and closes, and they are gone.

"What the hell ?" I say into Charlies hand.

Charlie pulls me close and points to the bear. "Look there's a bug. I'm going to call the landlord and have him exterminate this place again." Charlie is still holding me tight, with his hand over my mouth as he speed dials someone.

I am so close I can here the man on the other end say hello.

Charlie acts indignant, "Mr Williams, this is Charlie. You know your new tenant upstairs in Number Four. Pause. Yes, I am fine, except we have bugs in here, and I want them exterminated soon." There is a pause. "Now is great, we will go out for lunch and a walk. We will be gone about two hours. Pause. Yes, thank you. Bye." Charlie hangs up the phone and turns to me. "Let's go. He is going to come now."

I nod and get my backpack. I open it and search for my keys. I can't find them, so I just dump the backpack out. No keys! I look at Charlie, and he searches with me. Wallet, lipstick, hairbrush, two books, notebook, but no keys.

"What is the black thing? " I hold it up and just wrinkle my nose.

I barely have time to see the lipstick look-alike when Charlie snatches it away. He lays it on the table, looks at me, and takes my backpack.

I am pissed. "Can't a girl—"

I don't get to finish my sentence because he kisses me, then puts his finger over my mouth. "This backpack has a broken zipper. Let's look for another while we are out."

He points to the thing that lays on the table. It isn't mine. He beckons me to answer.

I stand there a moment and then answer. "Okay a new backpack would be nice."

No keys in the backpack, but a new lipstick thing really worries me, and I can see Charlie is worried too.

"What does that mean? Where did the keys go?"

Charlie can see the anxiety written all over my face. I search all over, this apartment. It is too small to really lose them here. Had I left my backpack somewhere unattended that someone could get into it —crap. I left it on the floor by the other student's stuff, then went to the changing area for rehearsal. I need to tell Charlie.

When we are in the car, and on our way to who knows where, I ask "What was that black thing, that kind of looked like lipstick in my backpack? Oh, Charlie you need to know that I left my backpack in the changing area unattended for about twenty minutes."

He turns a worried look at me, "Not sure, it could be a bug, but I think it is a tracker. Probably how they found us. I left it for Marty and Sterling to figure it out. I will tell them about the changing area and your backpack."

I sit back, twirl my hair - my nervous habit and ponder the possibilities. "I just don't get it. What do they want why? me?"

This feels personal. Caesar was possessive in Spain but that was two years ago, I can't imagine I am that great a conquest. Do people have egos that need that kind of satisfaction, I just don't know.

Charlie didn't talk for a long time. We arrive at Herman Park.

We are out of the car and walking before he finally speaks. "First, I want to find a place to put the blanket down, and then we talk. I am not able to tell you everything, but if you tell me what you know, maybe I can truly fill in the blanks this time."

That seemed fair, I know he is not my real boyfriend —it is his job —but I could sure use a real one right now. Eddie would be perfect. I want to just shout, "real boyfriend needed, please apply."

We spread out the blanket and sit down under one of the many huge live oaks. All over Herman Park, and on the Rice University campus, there are so many beautiful oak trees. If anyone is watching, we look like many other couples enjoying a pleasant day in the park.

Charlie leans back on his elbow and just looks at me.

I blush because it looks like he is mentally taking my clothes off or is it me just dreaming?

He sighs. "I wish this wasn't an assignment because I would do this differently. When I look into those beautiful eyes of yours, I forget you are an assignment, albeit a sweet one."

I look at him just as conflicted, "I am having the same problem. I picked you because you are easy to kiss and just be comfortable around. You as a boyfriend would be as amazing as any girl could hope for, but when the day is done, I am your job. Still, it doesn't mean we can't have fun."

Charlie cleared his throat, "Okay, let's get the business done, and then just have fun."

With a sigh of relief, "Here's what I know, or think I know. Dad, aka Whitey, and Mom, aka Big Bird, are working for some agency within the government that investigates foreign issues, probably CIA."

He nods.

"Next, I know they spend lots of time in Italy, Spain, Germany, and South America."

He nods again.

"Third, my Dad speaks Spanish, German, and some Portuguese. Mom speaks Spanish, Gaelic, and a small amount of German. I believe they are looking for, or maybe just gathering information about, the remaining Nazis, and maybe Castro's involvement in Germany."

Charlie nods again. "That's more than any of us, or your parents, think you know."

I smile, and then frown, "What I don't get is why me? What could I have or know that they need?"

Charlie sighs, lays flat on his back, and closes his eyes.

I am so tempted to come closer and just breathe him in. He emanates a manly sent, a cross between heady spices and chocolate. I know that sounds silly, but I like spicy chocolate. Just as I have made the decision to move closer, he opens his eyes and sits up.

He is wide-eyed and looking all around. "What's wrong?"

I jump back. "I don't know, is there something wrong?"

After looking all around, he says, "I felt you move, and I thought you saw something. Did you?"

I blush and look at him, again. I decide to just tell him the truth or at least my truth. "I can't keep this charade up. I am too straightforward for that stuff. I guess that is why I don't have boyfriends my age, I scare them. I just say it like it is, and it freaks them out, and they run the other way, well except Eddie. Mom, aka Big Bird, says never tell a man how smart you are because it frightens them. If they are smart, they will know you are and appreciate you. But that doesn't help with boyfriend relationships."

Charlie grins so big it makes my heart sing, and I blush again. Damn, when am I going to get that blushing thing under control?

Charlie leans in, "I have read all the intel on you, and I know all about Archie and Eddie, or at least what is written down. I don't mean to intrude, but I care about you, and I think Archie did and Eddie does? Is it too much to ask you to talk about them to me?"

I am silent for a while, but he waits patiently for me to decide. I don't know how to do this. I have never talked to another man who I find attractive about a man I am in love with. Wow—that sounds crazy, even in my crazy head. So how crazy will it be out loud? Can I even say how I feel as I look into his eyes?

God bless Charlie. He lifts my chin, "Look, I will tell you what I know, like I have asked you to do, and you fill in the blanks with whatever else I need to know."

I guess I was holding my breath because I released and smiled.

He started talking. "I know Archie and you had something really special. I read the notes from your handlers, and their descriptions made it clear your relationship with him was amazing. Everyone should be so lucky. I know you were in love, and I mean real love, not puppy love. When I read the report, I was jealous. I bet you think of him as your angel watching over you. When you sleep, you sometimes call his name. I am jealous of that kind of love."

I nod, and a tear runs down my cheek.

Charlie kisses it away and continues, "Eddie is the man who brought you back to the real world with the help of your friends' care. Even your Mom saw that. Eddie proposed to you before he left for boot camp. I think your parents think it is a promise ring, and not a real proposal, but I can't see that as true. All the reports I have read about him makes me feel like he knows what he wants, and it is you. I have seen you read letters from him, and I have seen you write him every day. I know you have changed a lot in the twenty-eight months he has been gone, and I am sure he has too. Vietnam is a bad place, and you see really bad stuff there. When he comes back, I know you will want time with him to reconnect. I have seen men who have come back. Some are ok and others are not. Every war has that effect, but Vietnam may be one of the worst. I hope for your sake, he is okay."

I have seen the two rings around your neck, and I have never heard you tell others you are engaged. I am not sure why, but I think you are afraid he will not come back, and you will lose another love."

I swallow hard and start to open my mouth to talk, but Charlie puts his finger on my lips and requests silently to wait. "

Emmy, this is the hard part for me. I am also in a dangerous business, so I understand the scary experience of losing of loved ones. I know you are my job, and I will be here for you in that way no matter what. I do need you to know you are not only a job, but I want you too. Do I have a right to push Eddie out of your life? No, I don't, but I have moments when I want to. Understand I am here, and I am yours if you will have me. I know that decision can't be made until two things happen. One, this job is done, and I am a regular guy in your world. And two, Eddie is home, and you have had time with him. Dang, that was hard."

I look into those beautiful eyes, and I just can't talk. How can one girl be so lucky? The tears just start to flow.

Charlie has been looking off in the distance while he was

talking, and suddenly, he just rolls on his side and pulls me close. I am surprised and pleased, but just as I snuggle into him, I hear him talk into a mic attached to the inside of his shirt. "I think there is a bogey at nine o'clock, about fifty yards away, by the swings. No kids with him, and he's just staring this way. It could be nothing, but, with the bug in the house, I am a little worried. I have Kitten shielded, but that means I can't watch him. Anyone have eyes on him?"

It was then I noticed the earpiece in his ear. I lean into him, I am shaking, and I trying not to cry. The shaking is from fear, and the crying is the shattering of the bubble of emotion I had fallen into just minutes ago. So, this is not just a job, and then it is. How do I know what to feel? Can this get any crazier and more confusing? I see he is conflicted too.

A few minutes later, a ball bounces onto our blanket. A guy came for it and says softly, "False alarm. Not our perp, but the guy is a predator, a pedophile. He was arrested, probably saved a kid or two by taking him off the street." The guy moved back and says louder, "Sorry, about the ball. Glad it didn't hurt anyone. We'll be more careful." He was gone, but I knew not too far.

I push away and sit up.

Charlie looks confused. He can see my anger.

I just don't care. I want answers. "It's your turn to talk and fill in the blanks."

He looks around. "Okay, I think I have told you how I feel about you. Well, what about us. It's hard to know how to tell you because it's complicated, and all this has happened over time, lots of time."

I want to talk to him about us, but he is right, Eddie is in the way and I need to work that out. It will take Eddie being here in person first to have clarity. Charlie is amazing, and I have fantasized about us, but I thought it was one-sided, and I am just his job. This is so confusing. But I can't move forward with *anything* until this Caesar thing is done.

Grow up, Emmy. Face this man and be honest. "Charlie, you are amazing"

Charlie "But—"

This time, I put my finger on his lips. "No buts. You are amazing, and I want you. The thing is I promised another man I would wait. I am confused maybe lost. I think I love Eddie, but, like you said, that was twenty-eight months ago when I was just sixteen. He has been at war and has grown up in ways I can't even imagine. But I am not the same girl he left behind. Can you be patient? I need to sort this out. Can we live just in the moment? Am I asking too much? Let's get Caesar first, then figure out what "us" is.

He smiles and nods.

I thank him with a kiss.

Sterling and Marty stroll up and intrude. "Wow you two make it look real with that kiss."

Sterling looks jealous or does he know something?

Marty cocks his head, furrows his eyebrows, and then smiles, "I think it is real." I look back and forth between the guys and wonder, do guys talk about girls like girls talk about guys? Probably.

"Okay, boys spill. What was in the apartment?"

Charlie sits up. "Well?"

Marty smiles that kind of smile that has a lot more behind it than just a smile. Charlie tilts his head, looks are exchanged all around. I don't have to be a genius to read that kind of look. It is simple, "Shut up."

Marty starts first, "One bug and a tracker, just like you thought."

Sterling flops down beside me, "We changed the locks since there was no sign of your set of keys, Emmy." Charlie uses his serious business voice, "Emmy and I were just about to go over some facts about this case, so Marty sit down and help."

Sterling laughs. "Yeah, we could tell you were talking because your lips were attached to hers."

I clear my throat and just start without them. "I know I have asked why me and not Lucy. You told me why—I am the easier target. I get that, but I guess I am confused. Why having just one of us helps them?"

Marty has obviously thought about this a lot because he is the first to answer. "Well, as far as we know, you appear to be a vulnerable, soft target who could be used to stop, or delay, your parents' assignment. The last encounter did delay your parents work and if that keeps happening that makes it dangerous for them. It'll also destroy all their work over the years. We think they believe if they kidnap you, then they can control your parents' abilities to locate people in a timely fashion. Your parents are close to their targets. They are not in this for money or intel, just to delay your parents, so they can hide their clients again."

I had guessed some of those reasons. But what are my parents doing that would be that important? They are loving, caring parents. "Okay, I could have guessed that. But that still doesn't answer what is that important? And, who are they?"

Sterling looks at me like I am stupid. "You told me what they are doing on assignment. Your parents are Nazi hunters. They don't capture them, but they let others go in and get them. They just find them. Your parent's ability to fit into lots of different social circles which enables them to get subtle intel to help locate Nazis in hiding. Some are hiding in plain sight. We just need to know where to look. Your parents do that well. The Rat Line wants them stopped."

I just freeze. I can't believe what I am hearing. I know from eavesdropping on my parents talking that "The Rat Line" is embedded in Spain and Italy. Their job is to extricate Nazis out of harm's way mostly to South America. I turn to Charlie "So, is Caesar part of the Rat Line?"

"We think he and Carlos are part of their more visible side? Caesar is smart and usually not on the front lines but for some reason he is taking a risk with you. He is acting like a man in love. Carlos is involved, but he is actually closer to the real bosses. Caesar will be a great catch, but Carlos would really put a wrench in their upper echelon. I know this is a delicate conversation. Your response to his attacks, and Karly, the general's daughter proclaiming her love for him, has us wondering who he is really focusing on. Well, I mean who he is in love with. I've always thought it is you. Looks like I am right."

Charlie looks straight into my eyes, like he could read my thoughts about Caesar. He just sat there, waiting for my answer.

I have no idea how to answer. Charlie is, rather or was, a fantasy. However now, but now he does want to transform our relationship in a real way, not a job. I know while I was in Spain, I *thought* I loved Caesar, but I think it was a young girl's movie/romantic fantasy. I am writing Eddie every day. I want to allow my relationship with Eddie to grow. That will not happen until he is home, and who knows when that will be. I guess I was staring to long without speaking.

Marty waves his hand in front of my face. "Anyone home."

I get myself together and sit up Indian style in front of Charlie, Sterling, and Marty. "I can try to tell you everything I can remember about Caesar and Carlos during my time in Spain. It sounds like my private life there is and was not so private. Maybe if I tell you everything I can think of and feel you can catch him or at least his buddies so I can go back to being a normal college kid,"

They sit up too, and they all just give me one of those sad smiles people give you when they know you have a not so nice pill to take.

Once again I have to pull up my big girl panties and survive. "I met Caesar, and how Carlos is who introduced me to him. Red introduced me to Carlos. Not sure how he fits in? Then, I remember Carlos was one of the guys who helped all of us with our luggage at the airport in Madrid when we arrived. I realize now I should have questioned how Carlos and his friends were at the airport in Madrid at just the right time to meet us and how they lived in the town we were going to school in. We seemed to be the only group they approached, and Red was very friendly with them."

I take a deep breath and a sip of my tea, "Salamanca is not close to Madrid, It is hours by bus from Madrid. So, I met Carlos there in Madrid, and then later he was at the pool in Salamanca. Carlos had a prearranged bride, but said he would run away and marry me in front of his bride to be. She seemed to be awfully young I mean younger than I was, maybe fourteen. He said his dad knew who my father is, and his dad would approve of me as his new bride. I thought he was just flirting. It kind of made me mad he would say all of that in front of his arranged bride."

I sigh and need more tea. "Oh, and Carlos and Caesar like to be in the social clubs at night, and both can dance— <u>well</u>, especially Caesar. It is why I initially was attracted—I like to dance, and so did he. I didn't fit in with the Americans who came to school together with me, especially the guys. I don't usually date guys my age. They just are too preoccupied with sex and can't put together two sentences that don't involve sports or sex. I guess that is what made me gravitate to Carlos and Caesar because they discussed more adult topics, like politics and events happening in the US and Europe."

Charlie interrupted me, "What happened to make Carlos back off from you, letting Caesar take the lead with you?" That question really made me stop and think. When did that happen? "I think it started the night Carlos whispered in my ear to run away with him for the fifth time in one night. That time, I could tell he meant it not just flirting, but with an urgency I thought was just lust. That kind of need and urgency frightened me. Caesar seemed not so scary, or at least not so pushy. I'm not one to be pushed into something, especially love or sex."

As I realize how candid I have just been with these men, and I emphasize men, I blush again. I mean I am technically sleeping with one, and the other two listen in, so I guess they are all there. This makes me perspire, no sweat. Charlie must have realized I think they can hear everything in the apartment, so he makes me feel comfortable when he leans in and whispers, "They can't hear everything because I play the radio softly near their security bugs."

Since he has told me that he cares for me, and it's not just a job, he will wait, so I can be sure and sort out my feelings about the men in my life. I am resolved to put this Caesar thing behind me. But, right now, I really need to just shut up. This is embarrassing. I look up and blush again. I *need* to stop blushing *every* time these men look at me.

Charlie really is learning to read me because he smiles, "Hey let's get some food."

I nod, not trusting my voice just yet.

Marty and Sterling head for their car and we head for ours.

As we head out to the cars for food, Charlie stops me. "Why didn't you choose Sterling for this wonderful assignment? I am not complaining. What started as an assignment has given me a new great friend, and if I am lucky, so much more."

I look at him sideways.

He is sputtering, "I mean I'm just curious. I understand why you didn't choose Marty."

I don't answer him, I can't. I'm not sure I can answer him so he would understand because I don't. I know he made me feel safe with the story about his sister. His kiss was amazing. Is that what people mean by chemistry. I look up and he is smiling with a cute sexy smile. He pecks me on the lips "Let's go"

SIXTY EIGHT

Charlie

I AM THOUGHTFUL AND QUIET THE whole way back to the apartment. It looks the same, like no one has been in here but I know different.

"Get your purse, so we can go to dinner. I'll get the car." I find my purse and hurry down the back steps to the parking lot is out back. There are five steps, then a turn, and five more. The screened-in porch is there. It is small, just enough room for a small table and two chairs. A few more steps, and you are in the parking lot, next to the garbage area. I am running down the stairs, but as I make the last turn I run straight into Caesar.

He grabs me.

I scream and kick and hit him.

Over Caesar's shoulder, I see Sterling and Charlie staring at me. What are they doing?

"Help me," I yell. "Caesar's got me."

This Caesar says to me in that sweet East Texas drawl, "Kitten, you are finger-licken good."

"What?" I can't think. Shit, I finally get a good look at him. This is Marty, not Caesar. I go stock still. What happened? I look all around, no car. "Charlie where is where is the car?" All the while Marty has me in a bear hug chest to chest. Charlie smiles, "Marty, you can let go. She's safe. Kitten, the car is out front where I *was* waiting for you."

Oh, Marty still has me plastered up against him, and he is smiling big.

I can feel him, and I mean feel him. Yikes, he sees I feel him.

He leans in and kisses my neck. He sets me down slowly. I slide down his front, and he sort of moans.

A second later, Charlie is pushes him aside, dragging me towards Sterling and out to the car. Charlie looks back over his shoulder and scowls.

I hear Sterling say, "Marty, you're a perv. She's like your sister."

Marty answers, "Speak for yourself." "

Marty really is a Caesar look alike. I really thought he had me," I explain to Charlie,

We head out to get a burger. Charlie is uncommonly quiet. I don't want to mention the elephant in the room. Really, I don't know how. We pull in and park at Whataburger.

Charlie leans over puts his hand on the back of my neck and claims me. I like it, but I think it is for Marty, who is in the next car, to see, not for me to feel.

I pull back, realizing he is steaming jealous and needs to apartment looks the same when we get back. I am quiet the whole way back. make Marty know to back off. Marty doesn't have a chance, but Charlie is showing his insecurity. Okay, I can play this game. I would have never been this brave two years, ago but today, I want them to know I can play this game too.

I climb over the gear shift and straddle Charlie. It is a tight fit, and he pushes the seat back. I fit just fine.

He is so aroused. My skirt made it easy to straddle him which makes his maleness push into my thin bikini panties. His smile is delicious and naughty. I suggest we go through the drive thru. He smiles. "I have a different kind of drive-thru in mind." He snickers, and the moment passes and so his arousal. "

Marty made me angry—and yes, jealous."

I look at him and remind him, "I sleep with you. What are you jealous of?"

We look at each other and start laughing, you know the kind that just won't stop. Charlie and I changed that day in a good way.

SIXTY NINE

Houston OPS

- Kitten situation seems to be in control for now. Travel plans for last football games in the works.
- New plan in the works for aggressive attempt to capture Caesar. Assignments are being developed.
- All will be in Georgetown house for Christmas
- Tiger will be at Patuxent Naval Station for a short time to Christmas shop with her aunt.

SEVENTY

Confused

CHRISTMAS BREAK IS COMING SOON but until then I have classes to attend and survive. The guys are great at keeping eye on me. I feel safe. Sterling is the funniest — and I am sure he was the class clown in high school and the life of the party in college. Art studio hours are usually in the evening. The Fine Arts building is not too busy at night, which is both good and bad. It can also be a little spooky.

One evening, during class, I ran out to the restroom. I don't know what I ate, but it sure didn't like me. The restroom is one of those big ones, because it is used for accommodating artists cleaning not just their hands, but brushes too. Cleaning painting supplies and brushes in there meant it is not always the cleanest at the sinks. This night, the biggest sink looks like someone has bled all over it. I am sure it is paint, but it looks bad. I am in a hurry to solve my intestinal distress. I guess I am there for a long time because I hear Sterling at the door,

"Em are you in here? Have you decided to move in? Kitten answer me. I'm coming in. Holy Shit, what happened in here?" I finally got a word in and answered him, "It's paint if you are talking about the sink that is covered in wet red goo." Sterling responded, "Sure could pass as blood. You okay?"

Embarrassed that he is in the bathroom with me. "Yes I am just fine. It's my stomach that is not too good, but give me a few minutes, and I will be out. Thank you for checking on me."

He chirps back, "No problem."

The door opens, and I hear a girls voice kind of squeak out. "Oh, I thought this is the girls room."

Sterling in a very sedate, smoldering voice answers very matter of fact, "It is."

I snicker.

The days with Charlie are the best. When he is with me, I just am and really don't look around too much because my attention is on him. It is hard to focus on class with this amazing man standing or sitting near me. My sorority sisters are so impressed by his attentiveness. Little do they know; it is his job. I remember, even though he says it more than that. Their standards for boyfriends goes way up after meeting Charlie. I wonder if he is just a boyfriend. Can this be real, or even Possible ?

Marty shoots me a knowing smile every now and then. It still creeps me out. He has never seen Caesar in the flesh When he does, it will make sense to him. Caesar is handsome, but Marty is a sophisticated handsome. I was attracted to Caesar, and I would be to Marty but not now. I am just frightened.

The next days go by without any serious issues or so I believed. Christmas break is almost here, and I would see Mom and Dad and Lucy, maybe other family too. I am looking forward to the holidays, even though I would not have a date for the social events or New Year's Eve.

The Cougars are playing the University of Miami in Florida December 5th. Usually, the team will leave two days before the game. The cheerleaders, mascot, dance team, and brass band usually leave just a day early, but not this time. We will all travel together. I am excited to travel to the game until I see the look on the guy's faces. Oh crap, I guess I am a problem again.

"I assume the arrangements will probably be the same as the Florida State game back in November so why the crazy looks?" I ask.

All three look at me sort of crazy, and Charlie hands me the phone. It's my Dad. He is going to be at the game, and then, I will travel with him home. I put together the final assignments for all of my classes and turn in as much as possible. When we travel with the team, we have a system in place with our professors to be early or late with assignments without penalty. Thank goodness. Charlie and I have spent countless hours together, and I really do like him. He is kind and considerate and I now realize how nice it is to just sleep with someone.

I caught Charlie watching me sleep one night. I look up. "This must be boring work if all you can think to do is watch me sleep."

He smiles, "You know, it is said that the sincerest form of trust and intimacy is the ability to really close your eyes and sleep with someone."

I ponder his statement before I answer, "I get the trust part. But, don't you think having sex might be more intimate?"

He leans back on his pillow, "Sex is a close second, but sleeping means you have surrendered your conscience life to the other person to protect, or at least join you."

I have never considered that at all. I will carry that idea forever. "Charlie, yesterday when we were talking about the upcoming game and travel, why did all of you have such worried expressions? Aren't we going to handle it just like the other away games?"

It took a minute or two or three for him to answer. "Going to Oklahoma, Mississippi, and Tallahassee, Florida is a whole different animal than Miami. That's because Miami is a fast boat to Cuba, through international waters, with lots of dangers, not to mention small islands that you can hide in. That's why your dad will be there. He wants to be done with this. He and your mom are tired of you being a target. So, he is about to lure the bad guys to him. He will be out in the open, in a very difficult place to maintain any kind of real security."

I start to cry. It is silly but it is overwhelming.

Charlie tucks me into him and his powerful arms, just waiting for me. His breathing is steady and calm. He smells so nice, and he is so warm.

I could be like this forever. I look up at him. "How much does Dad know about my day-to-day life here with you guys? I mean..." I just can't put into words what I want to say to him. Well, I know what I want to know. But, how do I say it without showing exactly how I feel?

Charlie snickers and looks at me from the book he had picked up. "Do you mean about you as my job? Or, do you mean me sleeping with you? Or, the way it is obvious to the guys we could be more than friends? Or, that can he tell I think you are sexier than hell? Because if you think I have told him any of that, then you don't know your dad. What he would do to me if he thought I have touched you is pretty scary to think about."

I am stunned, and delighted, with his candor. I move closer and kiss his neck, then his earlobe.

He drops the book and rolls over onto me.

This closeness to all of him is intoxicating. Is this wrong? I don't think so. It just can't be. Well, I just don't care if it is although if Dad walked in, I might be concerned.

We flew commercial to Miami, so Charlie sat on one side, and Marty on the other. One of the cheerleaders tried to get one of them to swap seats. Marty spoke up in his best East Texas drawl, "Can't separate us. We are a great trio, darlin'."

My mouth flew open because she is the big gossip of the group. Marty snuggles in close to me. Charlie just frown and puts his head on my shoulder. It definitely looked like I have two at once, and they like it. I thought the girls would be the talkers about this situation, but it was one of the guy cheerleaders who winks at me. Charlie must have seen him because he makes a noise kind of like a growl. Such a reassuring noise. Marty just chuckles. I close my eyes. What I can't see would not worry me.

As we got to the hotel, the female gossip cheerleader comes close and, in her sweetest gooiest voice, questioned me, "Is your threesome in your room too?"

Again, Marty came to the rescue, "Nope, it's a foursome in the room. Her dad reserved a suite for us. She's from a very, and I mean very, liberal family. Any more questions I can lie about, sweetie."

Her mouth flew open and she turns and goes back to the group.

I am used to being an outsider, so her rebuff is nothing new for me. What does surprise me is two of the guy cheerleaders strolling over to socialize while we wait for the band to get their rooms. Travis and Bill have always talked to me, but this time, they are high-fiving Marty for putting Miss Suzie Smarty Pants in her place.

Suzie is not only the gossip of the group but she also acts like she is a step above. As the Cougar Mascot, I am the odd one out on most trips, which put me in a room of my own, unless the band has an odd girl in their group.

The line to get room keys is twenty-ish people long, so when the concierge approaches Charlie, Marty, and me with a welcoming smile and keys in hand, the others really have gossip material. The icing on the cake is at that moment, my dad and his group of men, bodyguards included, make their entrance. This spectacle is so unlike my dad that I have to put my hand over my mouth to keep from gasping. He floats over, hugs me, and shakes Charlie and Marty's hands before introducing himself to Travis and Bill. They are openly impressed, and I am confused.

Charlie leans over and whispers, "Remember he is being noticed on purpose."

Okay, that explained why Dad is talking to the concierge and he is speaking loudly.

He wants to know if we are on the same floor and do our suites connect. Satisfied with the answer, he confirms the floor number out loud.

He turns to me. "I hope you got us good seats for the game."

I nod, hug him, and smile, looking around, trying to see if anyone felt suspicious. But the only people are the band kids and the cheerleaders who are still waiting in line for their keys. Hmm, who is watching and listening? Maybe staff?

The bell boy comes in with a cartload of bags. He hoisted ours onto the cart with Dad's stuff.

As we arrive to the crowded elevators, the concierge walks up and says, "Mr. Secretary, will you and your entourage follow me to the private elevators?"

The looks on my fellow cheerleaders and dance squad faces is almost funny. Well, this moment will change things now. While I have experienced this kind of treatment, I usually shy away from it at school. I think Dad does too, but today, we are on a mission.

SEVENTY-ONE

The Plan

THE ROOMS ARE GREAT, AND Dad is next door. He comes through the adjoining door from his suite to mine, and he brought his intel packet, his security detail, and the proposed plan for the game.

I am very interested as to who does what and when, but mostly, I am happy to be included.

As everyone sits down, Dad takes me by the hand, "A private word, please."

Yikes, what is wrong? He usually just says what he wants in front of whomever. "Okay, sure".

He drops all the paperwork on the table and immediately begins to hand out the packets to everyone seated. I guess I will not be in on the plan after all.

I follow him to his side of the suite. I turn to look at the room behind us, locking eyes on Charlie before the door closes. He looks worried, I am disappointed.

Dad sits in the big chair by the sofa. "I have a few things that must be addressed, and I have a word from Mom. So, let's get the personal stuff out of the way first, then the plan."

I take a chair and sit knees to knees in front of him. "Okay," It is all I could think to say. Maybe, I will still be included. He reaches out and takes both of my hands. "You know your mom and I love you."

I feel like my heart is about to jump out of my chest. Oh shit, this is not good.

"And, want you to be allowed to be an independent, young adult."

I feel my hands sweating. I am hot all over. This is worse than I could ever imagine. He never uses the "Mom" card without good reason.

He stammers and begins again, "Your Mom is worried about you and Charlie."

I swallow. I can see the sad "Daddy" look, the one that says he wants to be talking to his little girl, not his adult, well almost adult, daughter.

"Is there a you and Charlie?" His voice wavers, and I know this is beyond hard for him.

I am well past puberty and am an adult woman, but not so much in his eyes. Crap, I think he is sweating too. He swallows, "I mean, I know all three young men who are looking after you, and I know you chose Charlie to be in the apartment with you."

I nod.

"All three are grade A men. But just what does mom mean when she says, "You and Charlie?"

Oh shit, just how much does a dad need to know? I think vague works best here. I mean, yes, I am sleeping with Charlie, but we are not having sex. Yes, he—no—we are enjoying each other a lot, but there is a line I am not willing to cross. No, that won't work. Gosh, I have never even thought of having an adult daughter talk with him either. This is hard.

So, here it goes. "Well Dad, part of the plan is for Charlie to be believable as my boyfriend, so we do kiss and hold hands and stuff like that in public."

I wait.

He waits.

Okay, that didn't work. "Uh, you know you can't just kiss someone every day and not have some feelings. As far as privately, he is the perfect gentleman." God, I hope that was enough.

Dad sits quietly — I hate it when he does that.

He lets go of my hands and leans back. Then he finally speaks, "Well, young lady…"

Oh crap, that's not a good beginning.

Dad looks so stern but confused all in one. "I can be a perfect gentleman too and still have a girl in a compromising position in five minutes, so I guess I need a few more details."

This is scary. What do I say now? There is no way he gets *all the real* details. Charlie might end up dead.

He sees my hesitation and continues, "I could just bring Charlie in and used a different method of questioning, if needed. So, start talking."

Oh crap, I have never had this kind of interrogation before. Mom must be crazy worried. Deep breath in and get this over. "Ok Dad, I am nineteen and have been kissed many times before, Charlie is not getting any farther than I am willing to go." I think that I have covered it maturely, but if the fire coming from his ears is any indication, I missed the mark by a mile.

Dad takes and releases a deep, slow breath, "You really think that answer is acceptable? And, just how far are you willing to go? I know what I think is too far but I think your generation and mine are miles apart. What is far versus too far? Guess I need to have a man-to-man talk with Charlie."

I jump up, and then stop, and sit back down, taking his hands again. I realize this needs to be handled like his little girl, not some Hellion on a tear. "Daddy, I think you just need to know I am not having sex with anyone." I smile, soften my voice, " I don't have any plans on letting anyone get that close, not even Charlie."

I feel his shoulders slowly relax. I am making headway, I hope. "Charlie is the kind of man I think is a good guy, and if not him, someone like him is who I would want to be around when I feel the need to get married and *then* have sex." I take a deep breath and plow on. "The next few days are going to be hard enough without this kind of tension. If it makes you feel better, then talk to Charlie, but I know he will say the same thing about kissing and holding hands and embracing in public as I have."

Sitting here, holding his hands, and delivering the message he needs to hear in that soft little girl voice does the trick. Thank God.

He sighs and stands. He isn't ready for me to be the woman I am growing into.

The knock at the door breaks the moment. He smiles and kisses me on the forehead, and I hop up to answer the door, but he beats me there. "No, don't open that. You need to remember not to just open doors without thinking about who is on the other side."

He's right.

This time, it is the good guys — Charlie, Marty and Sterling, my good guys. I am so excited to see the fourth and fifth guys in the room are Sean and Clark, my hero's. I hug and kiss both men. I think Clark blushed, but Sean never shows emotion. Sean has worked for Dad and Mom for years and is always on top of things. He has been there for my dance auditions, my Woodstock adventure, and the bomb at the house.

Clark saved me from the recent kidnapping and arranged the 'boyfriend' detail since his cover was blown during the kidnapping confrontation. Clark actually cuffed Caesar once but he still got away. I know Clark really wants to be the one to bring Caesar in.

Time to plan. We gather around the sitting area on my side of the suite and begin. All the players are here, well except the leading man, Caesar.

It didn't take long to get the strategy from the basic idea to exactly the step-by-step plans. I don't like Dad being the bait, but as all six men say better him than you, Emmy. My hero's.

I hope this will be the end of a crazy time. I have come to think criminals are just bad people who have a destructive plan. Then, when the plan goes wrong, they become obsessed. That obsession is the best weapon the good guys can use. Caesar's obsession clouds his judgement. His obsession on taking me is the hinge to this plan working. Caesar having to change his mindset mid-plan to go for the big fish instead of me is where he will be most vulnerable.

With the plans settled and dinner finished. I realize I did get included this time, and now, I need sleep.

Both suites are the same layout except the mirror of each other a sitting area and two bedrooms so 4 bedrooms and 2 sitting areas.

As I stand and declare I am tired and am going to bed, all six stand too. Wow, six gentlemen.

Awkward moment when I realize everyone is watching to see who is sleeping where.

Dad is watching Charlie.

Sean and Clark are watching Dad, Charlie, and me.

Sterling and Marty look at each other, and then rescue the day.

Sterling says, "Charlie, you take the first shift, here on the sofa, outside Emmy's room. I will take the second shift, and Marty will take over from there."

Sean says to Dad, "I'm first on your side, Whitey?"

Sean retreats to the other suite, followed by Clark.

Clark looks over his shoulder and winks at me.

Dad kisses me on the cheek, never taking his eyes off Charlie, then leaves for his side of the suite.

Charlie gets a pillow and a book and sits on the sofa, Sterling and Marty retreat to their bedroom, leaving me there in the sitting area with Charlie alone.

WOW. That was really awkward times one hundred. But not as bad as Dad's interrogation about Charlie, but a close second.

Charlie, walks over, turns out lights, except the light he needs to read by, checks the doors and windows. Finally, he turns his beautiful eyes on me. He beckons for me to come over by the kitchenette, and I do. The kitchenette is in a nook that shields us from most prying eyes.

I am rewarded with a thorough kissing. Mmmm, so nice, and oh so naughty. Now, I might be able to make it through tomorrow. I tell him about my conversation with Dad, and he gulps.

To Charlie's credit, he says, "Your Dad is fair and powerful, but I can handle that kind of man-to-man talk. Your mom, well, she scares me."

I look at him sideways. Is this man nuts? My mom is five-foot, if that, and tiny. I know she can shoot, but other than that, I think she is sweet. Okay, maybe not sweet, but spunky. Gosh, that's not right either. I step in closer and am rewarded with another passionate kiss. I take his hand and step towards my bedroom door.

He stops me. I whisper come to bed with me for a while. He

shakes his head no.

After a plea to Charlie to come to bed with me, he kisses me again, and walks me to the bedroom door, and breathes in my ear,

"Lock it. The enemy is not the only one here tempted to get in."

I smile and retreat inside. And yes, I lock the door.

SEVENTY-TWO

LANGLEY OPS

- Florida team in place in Miami, hotel and stadium team will have their hands full.
- The three Houston OPS team will stay with Kitten during game.
- Big Bird and Tiger are at home in Georgetown regular team there.

SEVENTY-THREE

This Is It

GAME DAY IS ALWAYS 'HURRY up and wait'. This game is no different. Caesar has to think I am here and an easy take. Then, just as he is ready to take me, he must be tempted to discard that plan by seeing the big fish in a compromising place and change course for the big fish, aka Dad. The powers that be feel that Caesar's ego would win out and he will want the big prize, instead of little ole me. Those powers better protect my Dad.

I, rather we, expect Caesar to make his move at the game in the stadium, but nothing happens. I wouldn't say I am disappointed, but my apprehensions and anticipation were at 100 percent during the game. My adrenalin is well past full blast, so, the drop back to normal takes all the energy out of me. I know we will have to regroup in the hotel after dinner but before the win celebration.

There is an after-game victory party. Will I get to go the party? How will that work? All this is rattling around in my head while we ride back to the hotel on the bus.

Well, it is a big motor coach, and there are three of them to get us all from Point A to B. Dad and the boys are not in a bus but in the limo in between the second bus and third one. No security is actually on the bus with me. I am in the third bus. There are two police escort cars in front of Bus One. The football team and coaches are in Bus One, you know the important ones. Bus Two is the band and their equipment. Then, Dad in the limo with the guys. Finally, Bus Three is the cheerleaders, dance squad, and any others traveling with us. Two security cars behind Bus Three well, they are those black suburbans you see all the time.

I am daydreaming, sort of looking out the window but not really seeing anything. Everyone else is loud and singing and talking, happy over the win. I like to sit in the front seats because I sometimes get motion sickness sitting anywhere else further back.

I realize I am watching an accident happening in front of me when the bus driver yells, "OH SHIT HOLD ON EVERYONE THIS IS GOING TO BE BAD."

I don't think anyone heard the driver because of all the celebration noise, except me. I grab the back of the driver seat and the arm rest as we start to fishtail left, then right, then left again. This holding on is not working well, I am being tossed around. Things start flying around. I can barely see Dad's limo. Then, like magic, things clear, and I see Dad's limo as it goes left into the median with two other cars. These cars are not black suburbans. I don't even know where they came from. The bus driver is standing on his brakes, and I can see the other two buses getting so much farther ahead of us.

In another minute, they will be out of sight. They haven't a clue we are in trouble unless the driver just happens to look in his rearview mirror. In seconds, the turn in the road will shield all the other drivers from the chaos that is happening here. My thoughts are jarred back to the present problem when we hit something which causes the bus to tip over on its right side, or door side, we just slide, and slide, and slide.

I stop hearing the screaming because the metal screeching noise is everywhere. Red stuff continues to fly around and I lose my grip on the armrest. I am flying forward with all the red stuff. When I land, I am covered by it. It's not blood or bodies, well, except mine. It is Pom Poms and megaphones and shoes and blankets and bags, all in cougar red.

The noise is *incredible*. Metal scraping the concrete is not a pleasant sound. I guess it's like what I imagine a building sounds like being pushed in a Godzilla movie. I think we slide forever, but it's about a hundred feet. The laughter and singing went straight to screaming and even when we stopped the screaming didn't.

I have landed on the steps that exit the bus, and I am buried by the red stuff. As I burrow out from under two feet of stuff, I realize I am not alone. Two people have also rolled down with me. I have no idea where they came from, but when we stop, they get up and go back down the aisle yelling, "Who needs help?"

I try to stand, kicking away the debris and look cautiously out the front window. As I stand, I jump when I see faces staring back. After a heart-stopping second or two, I realize it's Sean and Charlie, kicking out the front window of the bus. As the bus window crumbles into little pieces, and I check myself for injuries. I hear three-gun shots in a row.

Sean, Charlie, and I instinctively duck. The bus goes dead silent. All I hear is voices demanding stay down and be quiet.

Sean and Charlie, both turn as one toward the gunfire, and Sean launch's back towards Dad's limo, yelling back at Charlie, "Get her, and call it in. Stay in the bus. I will be back with help."

Charlie jumps in and unbuckles the driver. The driver is alert and thanks Charlie but gives him a wary look. You just know he is thinking, "What the hell, and who are you?"

The driver then sort of crawls back threw the coach, telling at everyone, to stay down.

Charlie pushes me down, pulls his gun, and positioned himself in front of me. I am on the floor, pushed up against the two front seats. I throw my arms around his waist from behind and just sob. I catch my breath and come back to reality. There is another burst of shots, then nothing. I strain to listen for any indication of what is happening outside. Nothing. Dead silence.

Suddenly, the shots start up again. Screams get louder with the gunfire, and that's when I remember my dad is out there. Charlie has been on his radio calling in for help. I can hear sirens, but they are not close. Dad needs help. I want to do something. I start to get up —I need to go look for Dad.

I put my palm out. "Give me a gun. I can shoot."

He turns and looks at me like I took my clothes off —no, that would be a different look. Charlie just stares for a second, then pulls me in close.

I tell him, "I need to help."

"You are, by staying here, safe, so the others are not trying to protect *both* you and your dad.

The planning session last night gave me answers to just *why* Dad is so valuable. And why I am that valuable. Mom and Dad have found many Nazis who were being hunted. But, why now?

Dad explained Caesar and his associates are part of a large organization that arranged the escape and hiding of Nazis officials after WWII. Most of the head guys went to South America. That escape route had been in place for a long time. Men, and their sons, and now their sons, were trained to keep them hidden and safe. Caesar is the grandson of one of those powerful men in hiding. He really wants to punish Mom and Dad, and you are the punishment.

My parents have been embedded in the group for a while. Their job was only for intel and did not arrest anyone. Dad said he didn't feel Caesar was going to kill me, just use me. What kind of USE freaked me out. Sexual? What other thing would be in his mind? I am sure all those thoughts were running around in dad's mind too.

My parents' long-time, deep cover has provided intel, results, and many apprehensions.

All this flashes by in a second. I *feel* so safe, but I *know* I am not. Charlie is talking quietly to me, but hell if I know what he is saying.

Charlie must have realized I was somewhere else because he put his finger under my chin, and then just kissed me.

I melted and hung on for dear life.

He did too.

I whisper into his hair, "Thank you for being here. That was close."

His answer is shaky, "I was so worried. You are so important to me, and I don't mean as a job."

I look over my shoulder to see the bus driver helping people out the front window. For the first time, I realize the gunshots have stopped.

Then, this girl keeps saying, "You can't leave Suzie back there." over and over.

Charlie got up, pushed me deeper against the seat and floor, and asked the bus driver, "What's with Suzie?"

The bus driver looks at Charlie and me and just shakes his head.

The bus driver waits for the girl who wants Suzie to come off the bus too to be helped out the window, then says, "Passed."

I bury my head in Charlie's shoulder and cry. I don't know her well, but she didn't deserve to be dead.

Charlie pulls me back, sees my distress, then pulls me closer, and whispers, "It must have been her time. God called her home."

I cry again. Another loss, how, and when does this stop.

Charlie and I stand there for a while, just holding each other, until I hear my Dad say, "I am glad Charlie is here to help me do my job protecting you and consoling you."

Yikes where did he come from?

My dad's quiet tired voice asks, "Charlie, can I have my job back?"

I practically leap from one man to the other. I can't wait to feel Dad's embrace. We stand there and just breathe. Dad is okay, and so is Charlie. When I lean back from Dad to smile at Charlie, he is gone.

Dad explains, "Four men are dead, and Caesar and two others are in custody."

I am so happy to hear this. I really want to see him in jail, maybe even dead. He has caused so much terror.

The University requires everyone involved in any incident to be checked out by medical personnel. I knew that would take time, but I knew I would not be in that group, I would be with Dad.

The story continues in
GROWING UP IN THE COLD WAR

ABOUT THE AUTHOR

Cathy O'Bryan is a new author with 30 years experience in teaching Theatre, Art, and Competitive Speech and Debate. After years of reading, dissecting, and performing other works, she has ventured out on her own with this debut novel.